COLORADO
RANGE WAR

Other books by Howard Pelham:

Highline Riders
Death Canyon

COLORADO RANGE WAR

•

Howard Pelham

AVALON BOOKS
NEW YORK

Published by Thomas Bouregy & Co., Inc.
160 Madison Avenue, New York, NY 10016

Library of Congress Cataloging-in-Publication Data

Pelham, Howard.
    Colorado range war / Howard Pelham.
        p. cm.
    ISBN 0-8034-9750-4 (acid-free paper)
    1. Colorado—Fiction. I. Title.

PS3566.E38C65 2005
813'.54—dc22

                                    2005012912

PRINTED IN THE UNITED STATES OF AMERICA
ON ACID-FREE PAPER
BY HADDON CRAFTSMEN, BLOOMSBURG, PENNSYLVANIA

To the young men of
Slocomb High School,
Slocomb, Alabama.

Prologue

Angus Davis heard the riders when they were a half mile from the cabin, at least a dozen from the sound. *Evan Wells*, he thought to himself. He pushed back from the breakfast table and turned to his wife, Christina. "Take the boy and hurry! Take him outside and up the slope! Maybe you can hide there until they're gone!"

Angus Davis was a lean, wiry man with sunken cheeks. Thin brows hovered over dark eyes with a courageous glint to them. He knew what was at stake—his homestead, his future, maybe even his life and the lives of his wife and son. As he stepped onto the porch to meet the riders, he couldn't ignore the fear gripping him, but he was determined to do what he could to save what he had built.

Evan Wells, by far Colorado Territory's largest rancher, had been by a week earlier with several of his riders and warned Angus that he'd settled on W–in–a–Box land, a cattle brand becoming famous in Colorado. Oddly, Wells had never seen fit to file on the land himself.

Angus had come from Kansas with his wife and son and filed on the hundred and sixty acres surrounding what

1

was now called Indian Spring, and Indian Spring was the sole source of water for the Wells' W–in–a–Box herds that grazed the surrounding square miles. Days later, Evan Wells had appeared.

"Take your family and get out!" Wells had warned Davis on that first visit. "Take them and go or I'll run you out!"

Evan Wells had gray–green searching eyes and dark hair beginning to gray. He was sixty but looked ten years younger. He wore the authority his wealth and position afforded him like a mantle, and men stepped aside to let him pass, something Wells accepted as his right.

"The hundred and sixty acres surrounding this spring belongs to me, Mr. Wells," Angus had replied, standing eye–to–eye with the rancher. "If you wanted it, you should have filed on it before I did. Now you hear this, sir," he continued. "You may drive me off but, if I go, I'll go fighting."

Now, Wells had returned to make good his threat.

"What about you, Angus?" Christina asked. "Should you wait here at the cabin for them by yourself?"

"Ain't no time for arguing, Christina! Get moving! Get up there and get yourself and the boy well hid!"

Her heart racing, Christina Davis ran to the rickety bureau in the living room, pulled out a drawer, and stuffed the small leather bag containing what little money they had into her apron pocket. In case the Wells crew ransacked the house, she didn't want them to find the money.

"Come on Walt!" she commanded and, grabbing her son's hand, fled out the back door, stopping only when they reached the scrub oaks at the crest of the ridge. Crouching beneath the oaks, Christina watched at least a dozen riders led by Evan Wells pull up before the cabin.

"You were warned, Davis!" Evan Wells yelled. "Now come on out and take your medicine!"

Angus Davis stepped from the cabin, rifle before him, barrel pointed downward. "Get off my land, Mr. Wells!" he ordered. "I won't tell you twice!"

Suddenly, a rider twirling a lasso spurred his horse forward. Before Angus Davis could bring his rifle up, the rope noose settled over his head and shoulders, and the rifle clattered to the ground.

"The least you could do is face me man–to–man!" Angus Davis shouted as he struggled against the rope.

"Get on with the hanging, boys!" Evan Wells commanded.

Fighting the rope, Angus Davis was dragged to a nearby cottonwood. Throwing the rope over a limb, the rider wrapped it around the horn of his saddle and backed his horse up a few steps.

"Get down, Thompson, and put that rope around his neck!" Evan Wells ordered.

A rider swung from his saddle and carried out Wells' command.

"Now hang 'im high, Hosford!" Evan Wells shouted to the man who had roped Davis.

Ten–year–old Walt Davis, crouched among the trees beside his mother, would always retain the mental picture of his father's body swinging back and forth beneath the cottonwood.

"Now set fire to everything!" Evan Wells ordered. "And find the gnat and his ma! We don't want to leave anyone alive to tell of the day's work!"

A man with a torch fired the cabin, while the rest waited for Davis' wife and boy to emerge. "Spread out and find 'em!" Wells ordered when no one emerged from the burning building.

"Come on!" Christina whispered to Walt, awfully glad now that she had taken the money. There could be no return to the ranch now, for Evan Wells would shoot both she and Walt on sight. Hand in hand, the two fled on foot across the prairie toward Prentiss, the nearest town, to start a new life where Evan Wells would never find them.

Chapter One

F*ourteen years later . . .*

Walt Davis rode up the slope and with slight pressure on the reins brought the dun to a halt. The sun, directly overhead, hit his neck and shoulders and felt hot enough to burn as he pulled the grulla horse into the grove of scrub oak and looked down into the valley at the knee-high grass and lone cottonwood. He had last stood on this spot as a frightened ten–year–old boy and, for a moment, the picture of his father's body swinging from the limb of the cottonwood came to him as clearly as he'd seen it that fateful morning.

The season was early spring, and the half-grown leaves of the oaks on the ridge were a velvety green. In the distance the blue outline of the Rocky Mountains was like a wavering line along the horizon. Gently easing the grulla down the slope, Walt pulled up beneath the cottonwood and stepped down.

Walt Davis was twenty–four, a quiet man of rangy build with brown hair bleached white at the ends from the sun. He weighed a hundred and seventy, most of those pounds in his broad shoulders and muscular arms.

Outdoor living had burned his face brown, and the dark face contrasted dramatically with his sky-blue eyes. He wore a faded blue shirt, faded jeans, a dusty, flat-brimmed hat, and half-length boots.

The belt around his waist was stuffed with .45 bullets for both the .45 Peacemaker on his hip and the Winchester in the saddle scabbard. That the guns were calibered for the same bullets was no accident. In a pinch, a man could make a mistake and grab the wrong bullets. With both guns shooting the same caliber, there was no chance for a mistake.

The Winchester, the latest manufacture, fired fifteen rounds, and Walt considered the Peacemaker the best revolver ever made. The gun was well balanced and a second shot was quick and easy. The black rubber grip was a comfortable fit for his hand.

Walt, growing restless, had resigned from the deputy marshal's job he'd had in Salinas, Kansas for four years and ridden west. Walt had wanted to return to Colorado for years, but his mother, heartbroken and always fearful after that ill-fated day in which she had watched her husband hanged, had made Walt promise to never return. Now Christina Davis lay at rest in a Salinas, Kansas cemetery and would never know that Walt had returned to Colorado to find and face his father's killers.

Walt glanced at the sun. It was about noon on a nice day, and he was hungry. Swinging down, he stripped the grulla of his gear and staked him out to graze, the tie rope long enough for him to reach water flowing from the spring on the slope above. He did the same with the spotted mare that carried his pack.

Gathering a fallen limb, he soon had a small fire going between a couple of rocks. Then he took a frying pan, a can of beans, a half side of smoked bacon, and a coffeepot from his warbag. Filling the pot from the stream, he set it beside the fire and set the frying pan on the rocks. With his skinning knife he sliced a few strips of bacon into the pan. When the bacon strips were crisp, he forked them into a tin plate, opened the beans, and emptied them into the bacon grease. He then dropped a handful of coffee into the boiling pot. A moment later, he took the pot from the stones and let the grounds settle. Now he sat with his back to the trunk of the cottonwood and ate.

He was halfway finished with his meal when he saw the rider. Remembering he was on land now claimed by Evan Wells, he slipped the loop from the Peacemaker's hammer and made sure the gun was loose in the holster. Then he watched the smallish rider come in. *A boy? No, a woman!*

She rode a palomino mare with mane and tail almost the color of her own hair. Walt noted the W–in–a–Box brand as she rode in.

"Whoa, Checkers," the girl said to the pony and, looking as comfortable on a horse as any cowboy, she pulled up a few yards out.

She wore a brown riding skirt, a tan blouse, and smallish brown riding boots. A wide brimmed white hat with a green ribbon for band rode the back of her head atop her shoulder-length hair. She had brown eyes with dark lashes and dark brows. The nose was delicate, the cheeks slightly dusted with freckles. Her lips were compressed with disapproval, the delicate jaws firmly set.

"Who are you and what're you doing here?" she asked.

"The name is Walt Davis, and I'm riding through." Walt set his plate aside, rose, and removed his hat. "And you?"

"Misty Wells," came the reply. "And you better not let my uncle catch you trespassing. He has no patience for fiddle–foots. He'd send you packing."

The name startled Walt. "Evan Wells is your uncle?" he asked.

"Yes, and he's always looking for riders. Are you interested in work?"

"Not at the moment," Walt replied. "I'll be moving on as soon as I finish my meal. How big is Prentiss now?" he asked, remembering the small town he and his parents had sometimes visited on Saturdays to buy supplies and visit with their far-flung neighbors.

"Not large, but it's a nice town," Misty Wells said. "If you ride east, you can't miss it."

"Thanks."

"Don't mention it."

Turning her horse about, Misty Wells rode southeast toward the W–in–a–Box headquarters. Walt sat against the tree and reached for his plate. Misty Wells was one of the prettiest girls he'd ever seen, he decided. Too bad she was the niece of Evan Wells, the man who had ordered his father hanged.

Walt rode into Prentiss a little before dark. The Wells girl had been right. The town was still small with most of the same businesses Walt recalled: mercantile, bank, cafe, laundry, barbershop, blacksmith, livery, and two saloons. The saloons, the Golden Bucket and Riley's, faced each other across a wide, dusty street.

A couple of horses wearing the W-in-a-Box brand were tied up before the Golden Bucket. Walt, not trusting himself where men from the W–in–a–Box were concerned, and not wanting to show his hand so soon, decided to try Riley's.

At that moment the doors of the Golden Bucket were thrown open, and a man came flying out feet first and landed in the dusty street. Two men followed, stopping beside the man whose nose was smashed, his face bruised and bleeding.

"You dirty snakes!" he shouted at his assailants. "You jump me one at a time, and I'll show you what for!"

The younger man was intent on delivering more punishment. He was maybe twenty-five and what most women would have called handsome: blond hair, square face, and intense gray eyes. He wore light gray pants and a matching Western shirt, a dark coat, well shined black boots, and a black silk kerchief about his neck.

"Shut up!" the younger man sneered. "Shut up, or I'll kick you all the way into next week!"

Walt had never been able to watch either man or animal abused. "Step back," he ordered. "The man's down and looks whipped already. You kick him again, and I'll deal myself in."

Surprised, the younger man turned to stare at Walt. "You stay out of this, stranger. It's none of your business."

"I ain't no stranger to these parts, son. The name's Walt Davis, and I said back up!"

Ignoring the order, the youngster lifted a boot and gave the downed man a hard kick to his side.

Walt put a bullet an inch from his boot heel. "I'll put the next one in your leg if you kick him again," he added.

Swearing, the man moved back, his youthful, handsome face flooded with anger, his hand lingering just over his six-gun.

"Don't do it!" Walt said, his voice calm but carrying to the far sides of the street.

"You got the nerve to holster that gun and make it an even draw?" the young man asked.

Walt holstered the Peacemaker.

Seeing the youngster drop into a crouch and his hand descend, Walt drew, hardly aware of his own movement. The Peacemaker bucked against his palm and bright orange blossomed from its muzzle. The youngster gave a loud grunt and, as he went down, squeezed off a shot that nipped Walt's shoulder. Then he slowly folded and fell into the dusty street, a look of incredulity on his face.

From the corner of his eye, Walt saw the hand of the second man drop to this gun. "Don't!" Walt ordered, turning the Peacemaker on him.

The second man was older and far more dangerous looking. Lean and wiry, he wore a tied down gun. He had a pale face and deep set eyes beneath barely visible brows. The eyes looked curiously unalive, a little like the blank stare of a snake. Walt had seen others like him, had faced them on the dusty streets of Salinas. Undoubtedly the man was a gun slick, and Walt braced for another showdown. Instead, the gunman strode to the Golden Bucket's hitchrack and swung into the saddle of one of the W-in-a-Box horses. He raked the poor devil's sides with his spurs and sent him hard down the street.

"That was Ace Hawley," an onlooker said. "He's Evan Wells' fastest gun. Don't think you're finished with him, stranger. He'll come back with his boss and a dozen riders. I'd ride fast and far if I were you."

"It was a fair killing," the old man who had been kicked said, pushing himself up. "This gent warned him. Anybody disagree with that?"

"That won't make no difference," another onlooker said. "Both of you better get out of Prentiss. That boy lying there is Evan Wells' only son."

"He's right," the old man said. "We better ride. Ford Wells wasn't much, but he was everything to his father. His old man won't be long in getting here. My name, by the way, is Hank Green." He extended a hand to Walt. "I thank you for your help."

"Walt Davis."

They shook.

"How bad are you hurt?" Green asked, looking at the blood seeping through the sleeve of Walt's shirt. Stepping forward, Green quickly unbuttoned the shirt to reveal his shoulder and examined the wound. "Just a scratch," he said. "Now we better ride."

"First, I best see the sheriff about this," Walt said.

"Then you'll have to ride clear to Denver. That's the nearest place you'll find any law."

"Don't think I'd care to make that long a ride," Walt replied.

Walt strode to where he'd left the grulla and swung into the saddle. "Which way?" he asked Hank.

"West . . . toward the mountains," the old man said. "My place is pretty well forted up," he added, climbing astride his own mount. "Wells will think twice before coming after us there."

"You got trouble of your own with Wells?" Walt asked.

"He's been after my place for years, but I won't sell to him. Reckon he thinks if his men keep messing with me, I'll change my mind."

The old man's words brought back the troubles Walt's father had had with Wells. As the two rode toward the mountains, Walt considered the situation. Without knowing who he was, he'd killed Evan Wells' son. Did that settle the score? Maybe, but he knew the choice wasn't his anymore. Evan Wells would call the shots now.

Chapter Two

A half mile outside Prentiss, they rode past two women washing clothes at the edge of a small stream. One was middle–aged. The other was maybe fifteen or sixteen, with a figure that promised to burst out of the thin, cotton dress that stretched tight over her breasts and hips.

"The widow Barry and her daughter, Maudie," Green said. "Mrs. Barry is a good woman, but she's had some setbacks."

"Such as?" Walt asked.

"Dayton Barry owned a little ranch. He got himself throwed from a horse. Broke his neck. The bank had a note on the ranch. When the widow couldn't pay, the bank fore-closed. Her and the girl take in washing for a living now."

"Who owns the bank?" asked Walt.

"Guess."

"Evan Wells."

"You got it right the first time," Green said.

The girl stood and watched them pass. Walt met her gaze and saw only hopelessness and longing. Here was a girl desperate for a different sort of life. *Hope her ma's got a good firm grip on her*, he thought to himself.

They reached Hank Green's cabin a little before sundown. The approach was up a steep grade, and the cabin was set against the side of a mountain cliff that ran straight up a couple hundred feet. An overhang protected the cabin from falling rocks and debris. The building was surrounded by thinly dispersed alder and pines.

Built of logs, the cabin looked neat and sturdy. Smaller logs formed the base of a foot-thick sod roof on which various plants and vines grew that would have provided grazing for a small herd of goats.

The front doorway was offset to the right, and a four-pane glass window flanked it on the left. The door, hung with leather hinges, scraped the hard-packed clay floor when Hank pushed it open and stepped back for Walt to enter.

The cabin was one medium–sized room with a stone fireplace in the center of the back wall. On a mantel over the fireplace sat a large clock whose tick was steady and loud in the room.

"Belonged to my wife and keeps me company," Hank Green said, following Walt's glance.

Flanking the clock were two brightly polished silver candle holders. Both held partially burned candles. Against the wall to the right of the fireplace were two bunk beds, an upper and a lower. Leather thongs, woven together and tied to each side of the bunks, served as mattresses. Each bunk had a colorful Indian blanket at one end and a pillow at the other. Against the wall opposite the bunks was a small rock shelf which held a stack of books.

Walt was no reading man, but he had respect for any man who was. Stepping to the table, he looked at the titles . . . *Travels* by William Bartram, *Commerce of the Plains* by Josiah Gregg, *Three Years Among the Apaches* by Nelson Lee, *Journal* by Lewis and Clark, *A Tour of the Prairies* by Washington Irving, and *Oliver Twist* by

Charles Dickens. Except for the last title, all were books that taught men about the West.

"Reckon I'd better cook us up a little supper," Green said as he knelt at the fireplace to get a fire going.

"I'd be glad to help," Walt offered.

"Naw, you go ahead. Might take a look around outside, just in case. I'll fry up a couple of elk steaks, stew some potatoes, and make coffee. Won't take but a few minutes."

"Then I'll take your advice," Walt replied and went back outside.

The cabin was well placed for defense, he thought as he looked around. Except for the few trees, there was an uncluttered field of fire north, south, and east, and the cliff prevented any attack from the west. An additional advantage, Walt decided, were the slopes leading up to the cabin. If someone attacked, they'd have to fight uphill. Still, from what he'd learned about Evan Wells, the man had an army of riders. If Wells decided to come for him, he and his men could surround the place and attack at will. *Best I leave here, or I'll get Hank and myself both killed,* he thought to himself.

A boulder, worn smooth by the seat of Henry Green's pants, set beneath the spreading limbs of an oak. Walt walked to the rock and sat facing the valley, listening to the wind breathe through the trees. A blue jay scolded accusingly from the top of the oak. A camp robber hopped around before the cabin looking for a scrap of food and eyed Walt cautiously. A chipmunk suddenly scurried from a hole beneath the boulder, his tiny striped body a brown streak. Walt released a sigh, finding the scene ironic. Peaceful and natural now, but a scene that at any moment might erupt in desperate conflict.

"Time to eat!" Green called from inside.

Walt lingered a moment before rising, reluctant to leave the peaceful scene. Returning to the cabin, he sat across the small table from Green and devoured a plate loaded with elk steak, potatoes, and pan bread, washing the meal down with coffee strong enough to float a horseshoe.

"Just how good are you with that gun?" Hank asked, indicating the Peacemaker.

"I don't claim to be as fast as Ace Hawley," Walt replied.

"Maybe you better do some practicing then," Hank suggested. "Sooner or later, you're going to have to face Hawley. Evan Wells will see to that."

"Tell me more about your trouble with Wells," Walt said, ignoring Green's comment.

"Like some others, I fell victim to Wells' ambition," Green began. "I was settled on a little place next to the W–in–a–Box. Didn't think I was a threat to nobody. I was driving a few unbranded strays from the brush and slapping my brand on them, building up a small herd. Then Wells showed up. Offered to pay me a dollar an acre if I vacated at once and signed everything over to him, including my little herd. The amount he offered was far less than what the place was worth. I refused him, and that's when my trouble started."

"You mentioned your wife once," Walt said.

"She died back in St. Louis," Hank replied after a moment, something in his voice suggesting that his wife's passing was still a painful subject. "I had to leave there. Everything reminded me of Lindy and the plans we'd made. We had no children, so I just cut free."

Green was silent again, overcome by his memories. Walt, touched by the man's grief, waited for him to pick up his story, or not, as he wished.

"I had no idea what kind of man Wells was," Green continued after a moment. "I thought everything was settled when I refused his offer. Then a week later he swept in with several of his men and burned my place to the ground. I had gone out to hunt up some meat and was returning when I saw the smoke. I got close enough to see what was happening and saw his men scattering to look for me. Knowing the outcome if I tried to stand up to them, I headed for the mountains. Wells and his men kept on looking for me for several days but eventually gave up. Still, he took over my herd and moved some of his own cattle onto my land.

"After a while I began coming back into town for supplies and a drink now and then. When I ran into any of Wells' men, threats were sometimes made, but I never challenged what they'd done. Wouldn't have stood a chance if I had. I reckon I just lost it in The Golden Bucket today and tried to fight back. Guess down deep I been wanting to do that a long time and maybe was afraid to, but when you get as old as I am, your life don't seem so important, I guess. From here on I intend to fight back at Wells every chance I get."

The silence that followed was long and emotional. Hank Green's mind was on his dead wife and the loss of his ranch. Walt, drawn to the past himself, was seeing his father swing beneath the cottonwood tree. The stories were the same, though Green had escaped the hangman's rope.

"I get the impression your trouble with Wells didn't begin with you killing Ford. What happened between you and Evan Wells before that shootout today?"

Out of fear that their whereabouts might somehow become known to Evan Wells, Christina Davis had insisted that neither she nor Walt would ever mention to an outsider the tragedy of Angus Davis' murder. Thus, Walt had never before told the story. Now he did so quickly and concisely.

Hank Green was silent after Walt had finished. "I was lucky compared to what he put you through," he said after a moment. "How do you expect to go up against a man with so much power and come out on top? That's what you've come back for, ain't it? You don't stand a chance. He's got too many men and too much money. He can hire anything he wants done. He'll have you killed before you can get to him."

"Maybe," replied Walt, "but I don't feel I have any choice."

"A man always has a choice," Green insisted, "but I know what you mean. Think of it this way. You have to match his power and money with your wits. You have to be smarter than he is, always outthink him, throw him surprise after surprise. That's the only chance you have. And remember," Green continued. "Not only did you kill Ford Wells, you held your gun on Ace Hawley and got away with it. He makes his living with that gun. Now he'll have to kill you. If he were to let you get by with what you did, folks would think he's lost his nerve. Word would spread, and other gunmen would come, looking to fatten their reputations on Hawley. You've got enough trouble facing you, so I hate to point it out, but some are apt to come looking for you as well."

"Guess you're right," Walt said and thought of the decision he'd made earlier to ride on as soon as he'd eaten. That decision seemed even more appropriate now. What he needed, Walt thought to himself, was a place where he could settle in and come up with a plan. At the moment, Green's cabin didn't fit the bill.

"Thanks for the meal," he said a little later, pushing back from the table. "I guess it's time for me to be traveling."

"You mean you're leaving!" Hank Green protested. "I thought we'd fight Wells together from here!"

"I don't think so," Walt replied. "Until now Wells hasn't seen fit to come after you. If he sees you've hooked up with me, that will change. No sense in your getting involved in my trouble. True, you got a well built place here, but we couldn't hold out against Wells. He'd wait till dark and burn this place down around us or starve us out. You just make sure he knows I didn't hang around."

"But—"

"You take care of yourself, Hank, and thanks again for a fine meal. I intend to let things cool down some till I come up with a plan. Then I'll be back and finish my business with Wells."

Walt left the cabin and went to the small pole corral beside the cabin. He saddled the grulla and arranged the pack on the mare. Swinging into the saddle, he sent the stallion south. After he'd passed beyond the high cliff against which Hank had built his cabin, he turned west, heading deeper into the Rockies, taking care to leave as little sign as possible.

As he rode, he had to pick his way slowly. The slopes were high and steep, the valleys and canyons seemingly depthless. On all sides were countless varieties of trees and bushes: fir, pine, pinyon, alligator juniper, maple and small oaks. And he knew there were animals: mule deer, elk, bighorn sheep, bear, and turkey, besides the smaller critters, birds, reptiles, and insects. This was a rich, plentiful land. A determined man could make a living here.

Chapter Three

Evan Wells was the most powerful man along the front range of the Rocky Mountains from Wyoming Territory to the Territory of New Mexico. He had worked hard, planned, and pushed other men out of his way. Though in his sixties, he still carried himself with the military posture fostered as a major in the Confederate Army.

From a prominent Virginia family, he had volunteered along with a company of men from his home county who had immediately elected him their captain. When the war finally ended, he returned home to find both his mother and father dead from hunger and disease, and the plantation taken over by a Union colonel who'd had the land deeded to him.

Bitter and disillusioned at the South's defeat, the loss of his family, and the plantation, Wells headed west, determined to recap his fortune. Five years later, his brother, who had stayed home in Virginia, died and his niece, Misty, had come to live with him.

When he heard the pounding hoofs of a horse being pushed hard, he put away what he was doing. A horse in such a hurry usually meant trouble. Wells came from the

19

room he used as office and study, passed through the living room, and walked out onto the front porch of the big, southern-style mansion.

Ace Hawley pulled up before the front steps and swung down.

"What's happened, Ace?" Wells asked. "You trying to kill that horse?"

"I got bad news, Mr. Wells!" Ace Hawley said. "Ford's dead. A man in Prentiss shot and killed him!"

Evan Wells' face went pale, and he couldn't breathe for a moment. "What man?" he asked when he was once again in total control.

"Man by the name of Walt Davis."

"How did it happen?"

"We was rousting Hank Green, and this jasper stepped in. Ford told him to mind his own business, but Davis wouldn't butt out. He and Ford faced off."

Wells was silent for a moment, the only sign of his distress a tightening of his jaw muscles and something deep within his eyes. "Davis? I don't know the name. Where is this Davis now?"

"He probably rode out of town with Hank Green," replied Hawley. "My guess is they ended up at Green's place, maybe forted up to wait for us. Surely they know we'll come after them."

"Get a dozen men together," Wells ordered. "Be ready to ride in ten minutes. Saddle a mount for me, and I'll meet you at the corral."

"Yes, sir, Mr. Wells!" Hawley said, hurrying to carry out Wells' instructions. He was grateful Wells hadn't wanted more details as to what had happened, for Hawley was aware he had come off second best in the affair. Maybe when they reached Green's place he could redeem himself. At the same time, he began to toy with the idea of what the death of Ford Wells might mean for him.

Except for the girl, the old man had no other relatives . . .

Misty Wells intercepted her uncle when he returned from the porch. "What is it, Uncle Evan? What's happened?"

"It's your cousin, Ford. He's dead."

"Ford's dead?"

"Shot down in Prentiss by some gunman named Walt Davis," the old man said, pushing past Misty. Reaching for his holster and six-gun, he strapped the weapon on.

"Where are you going, Uncle?"

"After Ford's killer," replied Evan Wells. "I won't stand by and let a man shoot down my son without lifting a hand," he added bitterly.

Misty watched him walk purposely toward the corral where his mounted riders waited. She remembered the man she's seen earlier in the day beneath the cottonwood. He had called himself Walt Davis. Was he the man? He hadn't looked like a killer. In fact, she had rather liked him and been impressed by his courteous behavior.

Her thoughts were interrupted as the W–in–a–B riders headed west toward the mountains. They were led by her uncle, and beside Evan Wells rode Ace Hawley, a man she had never learned to trust. Everything about him . . . his demeanor, the look in his eyes, the confident way he wore his guns, the wariness of other men around him . . . all suggested a dangerous man. She had stayed as far from him as she could. Still, she suspected he often sought her out, for he seemed to turn up where she was far too frequently.

Nor had Misty been overly fond of her cousin. Ford had continually pestered her when they were growing up, even catching her in the barn once and tearing at her clothes. She'd fought him off then and numerous times since, and finally threatened to tell her uncle. Ford possessed a fear of his father Misty had never understood and, after the threat, he had left her alone.

Though his father refused to see it, she had known Ford

had a streak of cruelty in him that drove him to do brutal, cruel things, and she suspected just such an act was at the root of his death. But there was no doubt in her mind as to what would happen to the man who had killed Ford Wells if he were caught. Maybe he's fled the county, she thought to herself, and then wondered why she cared.

A few hours later, Evan Wells and a dozen men following drew up at the foot of the slope and looked up at Hank Green's cabin. As Wells watched, Hank Green came from the cabin carrying a rifle.

"That's far enough, Wells!" Green yelled "You come any closer, and I'll shoot you from your saddle!"

"We've come for Davis!" Wells yelled. "Tell him to come out and give himself up, or we'll come in after him!"

"Davis ain't here!" Green replied. "He rode out some time ago!"

"Where to?" yelled Wells.

"I ain't got no idea!" Hank Green yelled back. "Wouldn't tell you if I did!"

"Davis's in that house, boys!" Wells said to his crew. "Spread out, and we'll rush him! I'll pay the first man who gets a noose around the man's neck an extra fifty dollars."

With a loud whoop the riders spurred their horses up the slope.

Hank Green brought his rifle to his shoulder, took aim, and squeezed off a shot at the lead rider. The loud boom of the rifle echoed against the cliff and rolled out across the valley. The rider dropped his mount's reins and grabbed for the saddle horn. He held on a moment, and then fell sideways from his saddle.

The other riders, intent on earning the extra fifty dollars, didn't slow. Green got off a second shot but missed. Then the riders were on him and, flinging themselves from their saddles, were swarming around him, one slipping a crude noose over Green's head, another tying his hands behind him.

"Now tell us where he is," demanded Wells, who had ridden up after his men.

"I've told you," Hank Green managed, despite the rope that was already choking off his air. "He left here. Didn't say where he was going."

"Put 'im on a horse, boys," ordered Wells. To Green he said, "I'll give you one more chance."

He guided his mount up beside the horse on which Hank Green sat. The rope had been thrown over the stout limb of an oak and tied off.

"I can't tell you what I don't know," Hank Green protested, knowing he was about to die no matter what he said.

"I should have done this a long time ago," the rancher said and, taking his hat from his head, slapped the horse on which Green sat. The horse leaped forward, yanking Hank Green from the saddle. The fall snapped his neck. No one spoke for a moment, and there was only the creak of the rope as Green's body swung back and forth.

"Spread out and find Davis," Wells ordered. "We'll hang him alongside Green!"

A couple of men entered the cabin. Two others headed for the barn. The rest split up, one group riding south along the cliff, the other north. A few minutes later, Brock Thurston, the W–in–a–Box foreman, led the riders back to where Wells waited.

"Can't find hide nor hair of him, Boss," he said. "I reckon Green was telling the truth."

"Burn the place down anyway," Wells ordered, "and we'll ride for home." He glanced coldly at the body of Hank Green hanging from the limb. "But this is far from over. I'll see Davis dead, or I'll be dead myself." His hatred taking over, Wells drew his gun and emptied it into Green's body. "I'll do the same to Walt Davis when we catch him," he said and led his riders down the slope.

Walt Davis had ridden maybe three miles through the rough mountain country when he heard the distant shots coming from the direction of Hank Green's cabin and soon after saw the rising black smoke. His first impulse was to give the grulla his head and make a run for it. Then his concern for Hank Green overcame that urge. Turning the grulla about, he headed back.

A quarter mile out he left the grulla and the pack mare in a clump of cedar and continued on foot. By the time he neared the cabin, the fire had almost consumed it. Lowering himself behind a stump, he looked the place over. He saw no one. Whoever had done the burning was gone. Then he saw the body of Hank Green swinging from the limb of the oak. "The work of Evan Wells," he muttered.

Suddenly, he was ten years old again, and Hank Green was his father hanging from the cottonwood. Anger surged through him. He wanted more than anything to ride to the W–in–a–Box and have it out with Evan Wells, but he knew he'd find himself at the end of a rope or shot dead and, remembering Green's words, knew nothing would be accomplished. Finally, seeing and hearing nothing, he walked to where Green hung and cut him down, catching his body before he hit the ground.

He spread the body out carefully. He hadn't known the old man long, but he had come to see him as a friend and fellow victim. Hank had just decided to fight back at the man who had wronged him, and now he lay dead. Walt suddenly felt tears flood his eyes as he considered the old man and the way he had died. Something else for him to settle with Evan Wells when the time came.

There was danger in lingering, but he couldn't leave without burying the man who had become his friend. Finding a shovel, he dug a grave beneath the oak and, wrapping the body in a blanket, lowered it in. He filled the grave and stood the shovel at its head as a marker. About to leave, he remembered the books. He wondered if they had burned with the building. Walt found a scorched flour sack near where the cabin had burned and began poking around for what might be left of the books. He was surprised to find them intact, apparently protected from the fire by the stone cliff. Quickly, he stuffed them into the scorched flour sack. There was nothing else he wanted or needed, and he left the cabin and, passing by the corral, turned Green's horse loose. Then he returned to where he'd left his own animals.

"I'll be reminded of you whenever I read your books," he said to the memory of Hank Green as he rode toward the mountains, "and maybe I'll come up with a way to get even for you, my pa, and all the others."

Chapter Four

Walt had no particular destination in mind as he began his climb into the mountains. Having seen what happened to Hank Green, his aim was to find a place where he would be able to relax and come up with a plan to even the odds in a fight with Wells.

He made better time than he expected the first day, though the going was never easy. As he climbed higher, the terrain became more and more rugged. The valleys and canyons grew deeper, the peaks taller. Some of the latter, even in late spring, were still capped with snow. Often he dismounted and led the horses up steep inclines. The mountain-bred grulla had no trouble, but this was the pack mare's first time in mountain terrain, and she often labored.

Walt had never witnessed such majestic views as now surrounded him. The slopes of the mountains were often sheer, reaching high and losing their peaks in the clouds. He was amazed at the ability of various trees and bushes to find niches in the sheer slopes and put down roots to grow.

Beneath the lip of one crevice swarms of mountain

swallows had attached their mud homes. Newly hatched young stuck their heads out of the tiny openings, their beaks stretched wide to receive whatever morsels of food their parents offered.

Animals abounded. He saw coyotes, hundreds of squirrels, and birds in profusion. Both elk and deer grazed the tall grass along streams in the canyons. He saw both otter and muskrats and, at night, wolves talked to each other from the high ridges.

Near sundown on the fourth day, Walt made camp at a small seep in a narrow canyon. There was sufficient graze for the horses and water for both man and animals. While searching for firewood among a grove of aspen, he killed a sage hen. He roasted the hen over his fire and, using a small pan he carried in his pack for just such a purpose, made a thick soup, using wild onions, breadroot, and the bulbs of sago lily collected from around the sink. He ate half the hen and drank all of the soup.

As he ate, he watched as a high peak snared the sun. Soon the sun, as though wounded, turned a dark crimson, touching everything with red and leaving purple shadows in the canyons. Oddly, the scene brought the memory of Misty Wells to his mind, a girl he had met only once and who was related to the man who he sought to kill. Yet, somehow he knew Misty Wells wasn't like her uncle. Wrapping the remainder of the hen in a clean neckerchief, he saved it for breakfast.

Three days later, Walt led the horses up a steep incline near the Continental Divide. Reaching the summit of a tall peak, he peered down into a canyon. A small lake sparkled near the center, and a herd of deer grazed its banks. The Garden of Eden couldn't have been more pristine, he decided. The floor of the canyon was carpeted in green, and clusters of wild flowers ran the gamut of color from the bright yellow of buttercups to the darker shades of iris and violets, and the faint perfume of the flowers drifted up to where Walt sat the grulla.

"Now ain't that a sight, fella," he said to the stallion and wondered how such a haven could exist so high in the mountains.

There could be only one reason. The tall cliffs protected the valley from winter storms, obviously extending the summers and falls long enough for the plants and flowers to mature and shed their seed for the coming spring and summer.

Just the place I've been looking for, Walt thought to himself, and began looking for a way to descend the sheer cliffs. He had worked his way almost completely around the canyon before he found a ledge that led downward. A faint animal trail suggested the ledge had provided entrance to deer, elk, and other animals.

Stepping from leather, Walt knelt and studied the tracks. One print, a foot long and maybe eight inches wide, gave him a start. "A monster of a grizzly," Walt muttered. "I wouldn't want to meet up with him."

Leading the horses, Walt made his way down a ledge so narrow at times that the grulla had to be coaxed. The pack mare's reaction was even worse. When he reached the bottom, he stopped and let his eyes circle the steep granite walls that surrounded the valley. Their height dwarfed the tall evergreens that grew at the foot of the cliffs.

Leaving the pack mare to graze on the lush grass, Walt climbed into the grulla's saddle and began a circle of the valley, looking for a place to make a permanent camp. The deer herd—a huge buck, and several females, two with fawns at side—barely lifted their heads as he passed. Obviously, they had never encountered man before.

He found several possible campsites and finally settled on a cave that ran deep enough into the cliff to provide protection from rain and snow. As he surveyed the site, he saw the possibility of closing off the shelter by forming a wall with some of the slabs of granite shed by the steep cliffs. Closed in, he'd have a snug home that would provide safety from wild animals when he slept and would help to keep out the mountain cold.

He returned for the mare and led her back to the shelter. Once there, he relieved her of her pack, wiped her down with grass, and turned her loose; then he did the same for the grulla. The two horses trotted away to the lake, drank, and took a wallow. They frolicked a bit, kicking their heels high and galloping back and forth before they settled down to graze.

When night came on, Walt spread his bedroll in the cave and lay down. From somewhere in the canyon, a lone wolf howled plaintively. *I hope you've found yourself a good home too, fella,* he thought, *and a lair with plenty of food.* Then for the first time in several days, he slept without fear of waking to a gun in his ribs or a rope around his neck.

Chapter Five

Hungry for fresh meat, Walt shot a half grown buck the next day, dressed him out, and hung the quarters up to dry. Knowing that his clothes would eventually wear out, he saved the hide to be scraped clean during the coming days. He also spent time chopping and stacking firewood near the entrance to the cave, closing off the entrance with rocks and jerking the rest of the venison. The labor gave him a good appetite, and the venison was rapidly depleted.

Though there was plenty of meat in the valley, his supply of ammunition now came down to only forty cartridges. The cartridges, he told himself, should be saved for protection if Evan Wells and his men ever found the valley. As for meat other than deer, he wondered if there wasn't a way he could catch some of the smaller animals.

He remembered a trap his father had taught him to make by laying small tree limbs upon each other in a square with each successive rectangular layer an inch smaller. When completed, the trap formed a half pyramid maybe a foot high with a flat top. One side of the trap was held up by a triggering device, the other end, baited, extended well into the trap. The trap was sprung when an animal nibbled on the bait, causing the contraption to fall, capturing whatever had disturbed it.

Walt set about building such a trap immediately, using vines instead of the wire his father had used to hold the layers together. Since his need was for serious meat, he built the trap larger than those he'd built as a boy.

He set the trap beneath a wild pecan tree, a likely spot for small animals looking for nuts to feed on, and used a peeled wild potato as bait. He even went so far as to sprinkle an occasional bit of wild pecan meat in a trail leading into the trap. When he returned an hour later, he had captured two brown squirrels.

He was not overly fond of squirrel meat. They reminded him too much of rats, but he skinned and gutted them. They supplied him with ample meat for two days. After a week of eating nothing but squirrel meat, he used a bullet to kill a young buck. He had eaten Indian pemmican and, cleaning the guts from the deer, stuffed them with smoked venison sweetened with wild plums and chokeberry, and hung the lengths of sausage beneath the rock shelter to cure in the dry mountain air. With food to spare he spent the next several days reading *Oliver Twist* and dipping into the other books.

As Walt read and learned more of the world, especially the Western part of the nation, he found his understanding and vision of it expanding and changing. No longer did he see everything entirely from the perspective of a small-town marshal and cowboy. Instead, he gained more knowledge of how government was supposed to work and of the rules men devised in order to live peacefully together in a thing called society. Most importantly, he gained more of a perspective of where he possibly belonged in the total scheme of things. Such perceptions gave him more confidence and, at the same time, were humbling.

He also worked on the deerskin. First, he scraped the inside free of fat. He had seen Indian women chew deerskin to make it soft and pliable, but Walt couldn't bring himself to follow that example. Instead, he made a roll of the deerskins and paddled it vigorously an hour or so each day. When he was satisfied with the pliability of the skin, he made himself a pair of moccasins using the deer's sinew as thread. With the rest of the hide he made a rough, sleeveless shirt that reached well below his waist. Walt had never possessed a coat that turned the wind so well.

He was careful to observe what berries, roots, and nuts the animals ate, knowing those would be safe for him as well. And he kept watch on the pecan trees as fall approached, gathering the falling nuts before the squirrels burrowed them away. He made a habit of leaving a supply for the busy tailed little critters, however.

Since the lake was well stocked with trout, it too became a source of food. Like every cowboy, Walt had been taught from youth to carry fish hooks and line in his saddlebags. Though the trout had never learned to distrust a hook, they were still cautious. With their own food supply so plentiful, few took the flies with which Walt baited his hook. Still, he caught one occasionally, and between the venison, pemmican, and fish he was well supplied with meat.

Walt wondered how such an isolated lake had been stocked with trout until he saw an eagle fly over the valley and drop a fish he'd caught elsewhere. The huge bird caught the fish before it hit, but Walt figured other eagles had not been so swift.

He kept a record of passing days by marking each day off with a sharp rock on the walls of the cave. Though he might have missed a day occasionally, he still had a general idea of forthcoming changes in the seasons before they occurred.

The first real storm blew in from the northwest in early October, bringing rain, which soon turned to sleet and then snow, though what little fell in the valley piled up at the foot of the southeast cliffs. Walt's shelter, set at the foot of the westernmost cliff, received only a slight draft.

He had now formed a fairly snug room by piling boulders before the shelter, leaving a narrow passage for entrance and exit. Once inside, he closed off the opening with a heavy slab of granite. On this occasion, instead of closing the entrance off, he left it partially open to let the smoke from his fire better escape. Wrapped warmly in his bedroll, he settled down and slept.

A light cover of snow had settled over the landscape when Walt emerged the next morning. The snow gave the valley a striking pristine beauty. Walt was enjoying the scene when he heard the grulla snort angrily from a nearby grove of spruce. The stallion was answered by the high piercing scream of a mountain lion. Rushing back inside, Walt strapped on the Peacemaker, grabbed the rifle, and ran for the grove of spruce.

He got there in time to see the grulla standing before the mare, who lay on her side, a half-born, steaming colt emerging head first from her rear. The lion, crouched atop a boulder, eyed the mare and colt and defied the grulla with ferocious snarls.

Walt brought the rifle up and took aim but, apparently, the big cat either caught his scent or saw him. Before Walt got the shot off, the cat turned and scrambled out of sight beyond the boulder. By the time Walt reached the mare, she was in the act of cleaning her offspring—a male the color of fall wheat.

Walt knew the colt would never be safe while the big cat roamed the valley. Fearing as much for the safety of the horses as for himself, he felt he had no choice but to hunt the cat down and either kill him or run him from the valley. The cat's trail was easy to follow, and Walt stayed on it cautiously, knowing how dangerous a mountain lion could be when cornered.

The prints led into a huge deadfall of spruce uprooted by some past fierce wind. Circling the pile of dead trees, Walt found no trail coming out and knew the cat remained inside. He thought of burning the deadfall, but there was the possibility the fire would spread out of control.

Stepping back, he lifted the rifle and sent a precious bullet into the dead limbs. Luck prevailed, and the cat gave a wild scream and was then silent. Thinking he had killed the cat, Walt leaned the rifle against the trunk of a dead spruce and, stepping forward, pulled a long limb from the deadfall and began to probe. Suddenly, the cat scrambled from the dead logs. Snarling, his long fangs bared, he lunged for Walt.

Walt had no time to reach the Winchester. Instead, he drew the Peacemaker just as the cat sprang for him. He fired two rapid shots at the glaring, yellow eyes and heard the smack of bullets strike flesh an instant before the lion knocked him backward, landing on top of him, smashing him to the ground.

Walt fought desperately to breathe, expecting to feel the animal's claws tear into his flesh at any moment or the beast's jaws and teeth to find his neck. But nothing happened and, when his presence of mind returned, he rolled the cat aside and pushed himself up. He was wet with sweat and shaking like an aspen leaf on a windy day. Backing away from the dead cat, he sank to the trunk of a spruce to recover. The lion's skin, he decided, would make a nice soft mat for the floor of the cave. He had heard also that the meat of the mountain lion was some of the most delicate to be had and decided to see for himself.

Chapter Six

Despite the high granite cliffs surrounding the valley, the lake froze over in mid–January. Fish had become a major source of food, and Walt cut a hole through the six-inch-thick ice with the skinning knife. The knife was essential for his survival, and metal snapped easily when frozen, so he worked carefully to protect the blade.

When the hole was finally finished, he dropped a hook and line through and was surprised at the speed with which the fish took the parcel of jerky with which he'd baited the hook. The ice, he supposed, had cut them off from insects, their main sources of food, and they were hungry. He caught two foot-long trout, ran a stick through them, and roasted them over his fire. Thereafter, he visited the hole each morning and cleared away the ice which had formed during the night, keeping it open for daily fishing.

Recalling Hank Green's advice about practicing his draw, Walt spent hours practicing from every conceivable position. He had seen gunfighter rigs and studied them. Now he slung his holster low on his thigh, and rigged a tie-down so the holster wouldn't give when he drew. He carved the holster down so that the gun's trigger guard was fully exposed and soaped the holster for an even quicker draw. These were small things, but he knew that small things could give a man an important edge.

Each passing month Walt felt more at home in the valley. He had turned the rock shelter into a comfortable place to live, and he had access to a steady supply of food. He did miss the company of his own kind, but he reminded himself that, with the exception of a very few, he'd never had much of anything but trouble from men. He thought more often than he wanted of Misty Wells, and wondered why she kept popping into his mind. By now she knew he had killed her cousin and, no doubt, hated him as much as her Uncle Evan.

One day, tired of reading and bored, Walt decided to seek out the source of the small stream that emptied into the lake. When he came upon the crystal clear water bubbling up from the earth, he lay chest down for a drink and saw the gold-laced quartz in the banks of the bowl which the spring had washed out. He studied the dull yellow metal encased in the quartz for a moment before he began to dig at it. The quartz was so rotten he could pick the gold out with his fingers.

Walt had always thought of gold nuggets as like the little round balls for old fashioned pistols. The gold he picked from the quartz was more like rough, splintered chunks of volcanic rock except for the color.

The vein of gold-filled quartz ran away from the spring and deeper into the valley floor, and Walt worked for several days before he estimated he had gathered fifty pounds or more, a fortune, he told himself. He might have gathered more, but he lacked the necessary tools.

Months passed and Walt's mind turned more and more to leaving the valley. Possessing a fortune with nowhere to spend it added immensely to his restlessness. When spring came again, he caught up the horse he still thought of as a colt, even though the buff-colored stallion he'd named Cougar was now fully grown.

Walt tied the deer hide sack he'd made to carry the gold behind the saddle. He had long since broken Cougar to ride, and he climbed aboard and headed for the ledge that led out of the valley. Once there, he stopped suddenly, turned around, and rode back to the trench where he had mined the gold.

First, he scattered the quartz he had discarded. Next, he filled in the trench and piled several boulders over the spot. He was satisfied only when all sign of any mining was gone.

"Now if anyone else happens to find the canyon and wanders around in here, they'll never find the gold," Walt muttered to himself.

With that chore completed, he climbed into Cougar's saddle and rode for the ledge again. His mind was on the gold in his saddlebags and, carelessly, not on what was before him. Hearing a gruff snort, he looked up to see a huge grizzly blocking the ledge. Walt had encountered the bear several times, but had avoided trouble. Now the bear suddenly rose to his rear legs. Resembling a haystack suddenly come to angry life, the bear gave a growl that echoed ominously around the canyon.

Cougar gave a squeal of fear and reared up to confront the beast. Walt fell backward out of the saddle, and the horse galloped away across the valley toward where the grulla and the mare were grazing, leaving Walt to face the bear from his knees. Then, to Walt's everlasting relief and surprise, the bear turned and, looking a little like a roll of cured hay, galloped awkwardly back up the ledge, growling and snuffing as he went. He turned once to look back, apparently to see if Walt was following.

Walt caught Cougar up again but, before climbing out of the valley, gave the bear plenty of time to get away. He studied the horses he was leaving behind briefly. Hopefully, the bear wouldn't return, and the grulla and mare would be safe till he returned. If he never did, there was no reason they couldn't survive here in this secluded valley. Turning, he cautiously headed for the ledge again, but there was no sign of the big grizzly when he finally led Cougar up and out of the valley.

He considered going to another town, but he was tired of hiding. Maybe no one in Prentiss would recognize him, or maybe Evan Wells had given up the hunt. Regardless, Walt was tired of feeling like a fugitive. It wasn't as if he were wanted by the law. If he ran into Evan Wells or any of his crew, he'd just as soon have it out now and, one way or the other, get things settled.

Prentiss hadn't changed much in the many months since Walt had been there. As he rode toward the town in mid-afternoon a few days later, he even passed the widow Barry along with her daughter, Maudie, still doing laundry at the stream. The widow now looked more like sixty than her actual forty or so years.

Walt wouldn't have recognized the daughter had he encountered her in another place. She was grown now, her figure possessing in abundance all the curves of a grown woman, and she moved with a sinuous grace despite her obvious weariness. Walt couldn't help but wonder why a woman who looked like that was still taking in washing for a living, and he was struck with sympathy for the fate of both mother and daughter.

He rode directly to the bank and, swinging down, wrapped Cougar's reins about the pole. Retrieving the leather pouch from behind the saddle, he stooped beneath the hitchrack, stepped up onto the boardwalk, and entered the bank.

A customer exited as Walt entered, leaving the bank empty except for a teller behind the cage and a short, distinguished looking man who sat behind a desk to the right of the teller's cage. Walt couldn't remember having seen either of them before.

"What can I do for you?" asked Cass Houston, the teller, a tall youngster whose slender, bony body would eventually grow into that of a man. He appeared young, and Walt supposed he was being trained for the job.

"I've got some gold here I'd like to exchange for currency," Walt replied.

"Gold? How much?" asked the clerk.

Walt lifted the bags to the counter. "This much," he said.

The teller took a look at the bag, tried to lift it, and failed. He opened the top of the bag and looked inside. "Is it really gold?" he asked incredulously, fingering the precious stones.

"It's gold," Walt replied, amused at the teller's reaction.

"Mr. Courtney!" the teller called, getting more and more excited.

"Yes, Houston?" answered the man behind the desk.

"Maybe you should handle this, sir. This gentleman wants to exchange a fortune in gold for cash! That's Mr. Courtney, our president, sir," the clerk explained as the banker approached.

Richard Courtney was around forty, stocky, and maybe five-feet-six. He had little or no neck, and his large head seemed to grow directly from his shoulders. Known as a keen, intelligent man, he took a quick look inside the one bag and turned to Walt.

"Follow me, and bring that along," he said, indicating the bag, and led Walt through a door and into the rear of the bank.

"Must have made yourself a very rich strike," he said to Walt as he began to weigh the gold.

Walt made no reply and watched the banker examine many of the nuggets, testing one for purity from time to time. "Very fine quality," he said as he placed the nuggets on the scales. When he was finished, he crossed to a desk, sat down, and wrote out a receipt for the gold. The he figured with pencil and pad for a couple of minutes. "Comes to sixty–five thousand, two hundred and eighty–six dollars if the quality holds up," he said when he was finished. "But you understand I'll have to have the whole lot tested at the assay office before I can make you a price."

"How long will that take?" Walt asked.

"I'll get Seth Gumby, the assayer, on it at once," Courtney said. "He owes me some favors. Come back in a couple of hours."

Walt left the bank and, hungry, stopped in at a nearby cafe. He ordered a steak, potatoes and gravy, and coffee, dawdling over the meal until it was time for him to return to the bank.

"Well, my figures were pretty close," Courtney told him when Walt reentered the bank. "Comes to sixty–five thousand, two hundred and seventy-five dollars. You can verify that with Seth Gumby at the assay office if you like."

"No need, sir," Walt replied. "I expect I can trust you."

"Would you like to make a deposit of some of the money?" Courtney asked.

"Might as well."

"How much?" asked Courtney, brightening at once.

"Sixty thousand," Walt replied.

"A nice round sum," the banker said, unable to contain his pleasure at such a hefty deposit. He wrote out a receipt for that amount and passed it to Walt. "Houston!" he called.

Houston entered the room a moment later. "Yes, sir?"

"Count out five thousand, two hundred and seventy-five dollars for this gentleman," Courtney told him.

"Yes, sir, Mr. Courtney!" The teller turned back to his cage and, returning a moment later, counted the money out in bills for Walt.

"Now what else can I do for you, Mr. Davis?" the banker asked when Houston was gone.

"There is a small favor," Walt replied.

"You've only to name it," said the banker.

"Do you know the widow Barry?" Walt asked. "She has a daughter named Maudie. They live in Prentiss and take in laundry."

"I don't know the lady, but I have heard my wife mention the name," replied Courtney.

Walt peeled off a thousand dollars. "I'd like you to give her this. Just say a friend wanted her to have it, but don't tell her my name. Tell her she's free to use it any way she likes."

Courtney looked bewildered. "What has Mrs. Barry to do with you?" he asked.

"That's my business," Walt replied. "Will you do as I ask? Or shall I find someone else?"

"I'll take care of it," Courtney replied quickly, afraid the stranger might decide to take his money elsewhere too. "Is there anything else I might do for you?" he asked.

"I do have a question or two about a name I've heard several times," Walt said.

"A question? About who?"

"Evan Wells, the rancher," Walt replied. "What can you tell me about him?"

"He's the biggest, most powerful man around," Courtney replied. "He lost his son a few months back, you know."

"I heard," Walt said innocently.

"Turned the old man bitter and even more ruthless. If you've business with Mr. Wells, be careful."

"Oh, I don't contemplate having any contact with Mr. Wells," Walt replied. "I'd just heard the name and was curious."

"Come back here a moment, Houston," Richard Courtney called to his clerk after Walt was gone. "Did Davis mention anything about where he found that gold?" Courtney asked.

"Nothing, and I didn't ask," replied Houston.

Courtney was silent a moment, deep in thought. He had liked Walt Davis and didn't want to see harm come to him. If word got out about the gold, there was no telling what might happen. "We'll just keep our mouths shut about our transaction with Mr. Davis," he said to Houston. "No mention of the gold. Is that clear, young man?"

"Yes, sir. Perfectly," replied the clerk, Cass Houston.

Chapter Seven

Not having seen any W–in–a–Box men around town, Walt decided it might be safe to hang around Prentiss for awhile. But from what the banker had said about the death of Ford turning Evan Wells into even more of a tyrant he'd have to be careful.

Though he still had every intention of making Wells pay for the death of his father and Hank Green, Walt had no idea how he would set about doing it, having long since discarded the idea of killing the man outright. At best, that would mean a long stay in prison; at the worst, a hanging.

With a small fortune in the bank and more to be had if he ever needed it, this was no time to take risks, he told himself. And there was always Wells' pet gunman, Ace Hawley. Hawley would never stand by while his boss fought a gun duel with Walt, and Walt, though he had practiced diligently in the mountains, still wasn't sure he could match Hawley's speedy draw.

At any rate, whatever he did must be free of any taint of murder, for Walt no longer wanted to sacrifice himself

43

in his effort to bring Evan Wells to ruin. Wells' downfall must come as a result of actions he took himself.

Meanwhile, he needed a change of clothes, a room, a bath, and a good meal. He decided to begin with a change of clothes and so he looked around for a mercantile. Instead, he spotted something new to Prentiss, a men's clothing store a few doors down from the bank.

The clerk, portly, well dressed, and fairly young, oozed condescension at Walt's dusty, shabby appearance. "What can I do for you, sir?" he asked with a not–so–subtle sniff.

A skylight in the roof cast ample light upon the several shelves of men's clothing, and there was the strong smell of mothballs and new fabrics. "I'll just look around a moment and make up my mind," Walt replied, amused at the man's arrogance.

He selected underwear, socks, a pair of half-length boots, a white shirt, and a black string tie, and then passed on to the suits. The clerk didn't know whether to be pleased or suspicious. This could be his biggest sale of the month, but he remained distrustful of how such a ragged cowboy could make the payment.

Walt selected a brown pinstriped suit from a rack and looked at the measurements of both the coat and trousers. "You reckon this will fit me?" he asked.

The clerk reached for a tape and quickly took Walt's measurements, holding his breath most of the time to keep from smelling him. "Both should fit very well," he said when he was finished.

"Then you can wrap everything and figure up my bill," Walt told him.

"Right away, sir," the clerk replied reluctantly, still afraid of not being paid.

Walt followed him to the front counter and waited while his purchases were wrapped and his bill was tabulated. The total came to thirty dollars, and Walt took his thick roll of bills from a pocket and peeled off three tens. The clerk's eyes, seeing the money, bulged, and he gave a sigh of relief and became immediately subservient.

He thanked Walt three times as he escorted him to the door, delivering his gratitude with overdone sincerity. He reached the door first, opened it, and bowed Walt out.

Walt's next stop was the Prentiss Hotel.

"How long will you be with us, sir?" Sam Mitchell, the clerk, asked. Mitchell was a seemingly bloodless man in his late forties. He had bleached-out blue eyes and skin with the lifeless texture of parchment. A month or so in the sun on the back of a horse might change all that, Walt thought to himself.

"A couple of days, maybe longer," Walt replied, taking the key, "and I'll need a tub of hot water delivered to the room."

"We have a nice bathhouse out back, sir, if you'd like to visit it."

"How do I get there?" Walt asked.

"Go along the hallway to the back door," replied the clerk. "You'll find the bathhouse just outside."

Reaching for his parcels, Walt followed the clerk's direction and, a few moments later, found himself in a room with a couple of large wooden tubs from which drifted clouds of steam.

The bathkeeper, a middle-aged man of Chinese ancestry, welcomed him and offered him a towel. Walt sat on a bench near a tub and let the keeper help him off with his boots. Then, standing, he removed his clothes and climbed into a tub, pleased to see that the water was relatively fresh. He sank down to his chin and soaked for a few minutes. He then reached for the soap and lathered himself thoroughly, including his hair. When he was clean, he sat in the water and soaked for maybe thirty minutes longer, dozing part of the time. Finally, he climbed from the tub, dried himself off, and dressed in his new clothes. Feeling like a different man, he gathered his dirty clothes, left a tip for the bathkeeper, and returned to the hotel.

"Could you have these laundered for me?" he asked the clerk, indicating his pile of dirty work clothes.

"Certainly, sir," the clerk told him. "They'll be ready for you in the morning. Is there anything else?"

"No, nothing else."

Walt climbed the stairs and found his room. The furnishings consisted of an iron bedstead, a bureau, a couple of chairs, a throw rug beside the bed, and a window overlooking the street. He sat on the bed and, finding the feather mattress soft and comfortable, stretched out and closed his eyes. A moment later, he dropped off to sleep.

When he woke, the room was dark. From the street below came the sounds of a passing wagon. Rousing himself, he crossed to the window and looked down. Lights from a few store windows cast bright rectangles on the boardwalk through which people passed from time to time. An occasional horse with tired-looking riders jogged into town, stopped at one of the saloons, and swung wearily down. From the nearest saloon came the sound of a tired piano and the occasional burst of laughter. Feeling hungry, Walt decided it was time to find some food.

"Where's the best place to eat?" he asked the clerk, stopping before the desk.

"Do you like steak?" asked the clerk.

"Nothing like it."

"Then try the Beef House just down the street."

As Walt turned away from the desk, he bumped into someone. "I'm real sorry," he apologized and found himself looking into the face of Misty Wells, a face he'd often thought of during his long stay in the mountains.

She wore a brown silk dress that reached to her ankles. A wide sash exposed her narrow waist, rounded hips, and fulsome breasts. The dress was cut low, and a cameo brooch on a chain decorated the smooth brown skin of her chest. Her hair was pulled back and pinned to the back of her neck, exposing the delicate shape of her head. Misty Wells had seemed more like a beautiful young tomboy when he'd seen her first. Now she was not only a vision of beauty; she was also a full grown woman.

"My fault," Misty Wells said. Then she seemed to recognize Walt and took a step back, a look of concern flashing across her face. "You must leave town at once, Mr. Davis!" she said. "Uncle Evan and some of his men are here! No telling what they'll do if they see you."

Walt couldn't have been more surprised. He could hardly credit that she would remember him, and to find her anxious for him was even more of a surprise. "Have you eaten?" he asked, hardly knowing where the question came from.

"No, but—"

"I was about to step out for dinner. Would you join me? We could talk some more," he added, sure she would refuse.

"Could we go somewhere out of the way?" she asked, surprising Walt even more. "My Uncle Evan would never forgive me if he saw us together."

"Come," Walt said and, taking her arm, guided her out to the street where he hailed the carriage the hotel kept handy for guests. "What kind of food do you like?" he asked as the carriage pulled abreast.

"Well, we don't have too many choices in Prentiss, but I like Chinese. How about you?"

"I like anything cooked by someone other than me," Walt said.

"You know of the Chinese café?" Walt asked the driver.

"I've never ate there," the driver replied, "but I take folks to the Mah Fong sometimes."

The driver wore a black, round straw hat with narrow brim, a white shirt, black string tie, and a black coat with collar trimmed in red silk that glistened in the dim light cast through the hotel windows. Walt decided his outfit was more appropriate to a city like St. Louis than a small town like Prentiss, but maybe the hotel manager was trying to give the town some class. Still, he couldn't help but wonder how the man managed to survive the reaction he surely got from some of the rough and ready cowboys who drifted into Prentiss from time to time.

"The Mah Fong it is," Walt said, and he helped Misty into the carriage, which was little more than a covered buggy, but longer, with an elevated seat for the driver.

The driver snapped a whip smartly over the backs of the two horses, and the carriage moved out smartly, the metal rims on the wheels making a gritty sound on the dry street. They passed pedestrians along the way, mostly men, but a few doves of the night peddled their wares, some from doors or windows, others at the entrance to dark alleys.

Walt's face burned as they called out to him, and he tried to think of something to say to Misty Wells to distract her attention from the women, but he could think of nothing. In fact, he was still trying to figure out why the niece of the man who wanted to kill him would dare venture out with him at all. What could be her purpose? Walt was far too modest to think she might have even a passing interest in him.

"Is it true what they say, Mr. Davis?" she asked.

"About what?"

"That you shot Ford down in cold blood?"

Walt suddenly wanted very much for Misty Wells to

understand why he had confronted Ford Wells. "Your cousin was kicking a man while he was down in the street," he replied after a moment. "I told him to stop. Instead, he chose to draw on me. If I hadn't shot your cousin, he would have killed me."

"That sounds like Ford," Misty replied. "He was always cruel . . . and a bully."

There was obvious distaste in her voice, and Walt wondered what had happened between them that would cause such an aversion to linger even after Ford Wells was dead. Misty Wells was a difficult woman to get a bead on, he decided.

The carriage pulled up before the café, and Walt stepped out and lifted a hand to assist Misty. Her small hand felt warm and soft in his. "How much do I owe you?" he asked, looking up at the driver.

"A dollar," replied the man.

Walt paid him. "And here's three more if you'll wait till we're ready to go back to the hotel."

"How long?" asked the driver.

"Maybe a couple of hours," Walt replied. "Naturally, I'd pay you for the return trip as well."

"I'm at your disposal, sir," the driver said and reached for the extra bills.

Chinese lanterns hung from the ceiling cast soft light about the Mai Fong. The wallpaper, the color of straw which, in turn, was decorated with dark-haired, kimono-clad Chinese ladies in various stages of dance, contributed to the Oriental atmosphere. A walkway of crimson carpet led deeper into the cafe.

A lady resembling the figures on the wallpaper greeted them. Her face was white with a coat of rice powder, her lashes and brows as dark as coal, her lips red slashes. "Will you follow me?" she asked and led them to a table midway across the room. Prentiss, Walt decided, had made a step up during the past couple of years to offer such an ornate place to eat.

Walt pulled out a chair and held it while Misty sat. Circling the table, he pulled out a chair for himself. "Do you come here often?" he asked.

"Occasionally, and you?"

"I've never been in a place like this before," Walt replied. "I wouldn't know one Chinese dish from another. Why don't you order for both of us?"

"If you wish."

Walt paid more attention to the effects of the candle-light on Misty's cheeks and hair than to the exchange between her and the waitress. When the waitress left with the order, Misty turned and caught his eyes upon her, and Walt dropped his gaze guiltily.

"I expect you'll know me next time," Misty said and laughed at the deep blush that crept up Walt's neck to flood his cheeks.

Walt sought desperately for something to say to change the subject. "Do you miss Virginia?" he asked quickly.

"How did you know I once lived in Virginia?" she asked.

"I must have heard it around," Walt replied, not certain himself of the source of the knowledge.

"I miss my life there sometimes," she replied, "though I like the West as well. I love the mountains and the beautiful views, and women have more freedom. But I had more friends in Virginia."

"Do you hear from them?"

"I did in the beginning, but you know how it is. Memories fade, and friends move on with their lives. Eventually, our letters back and forth stopped."

"I should apologize for asking so many questions," Walt said.

"I don't mind," Misty replied. "My mother and father died of the fever back there. Left alone, I decided to join an uncle I knew little about."

"You sound as though you don't like your uncle," Walt said.

"I don't approve of some of the things he does," she replied. "He sometimes reminds me of the carpetbaggers who came to Virginia after the war. There was no law or government available for a time, and they just took whatever they wanted. The farmers banded together and tried to fight back, but they were no match for both the Union Army and the carpetbaggers. A carpetbagger took over my father's plantation. I only got it back just before I came out here."

"Do you still own it?" Walt asked.

"No, I sold it just before I left."

Walt hardly heard Misty's last words. Something she had just said had him thinking. He'd been trying to come up with a way to oppose Wells, and maybe she had just mentioned one. As far as he was concerned, Evan Wells was very much like the carpetbaggers she had described, and Walt needed help to fight the man. Now excitement built inside him as a plan began to form in his mind.

The food came, but Walt barely tasted what he ate as he struggled with the use of chopsticks. He was vaguely aware of Misty's amusement at his struggles, but he took no offense. When the meal was finished, they lingered over coffee a few minutes and then rose to go, Walt leaving a large bill behind to pay for the meal and a tip for the service.

The driver and the carriage pulled up before the café a moment or so after they came out. Walt helped Misty into the carriage, and they rolled noisily through the now mostly quiet streets back to the hotel.

"Do you stay at the hotel often?" Walt asked.

"Only when I come into town to do some shopping," replied Misty.

"May we do this again sometime?"

"Maybe we shouldn't." Misty told him. "Uncle Evan would pack me off to Virginia or some place worse if he ever found out."

"Good night then," Walt told her and waited in the lobby until she climbed the stairs to her room before he went up himself.

He stripped and crawled into bed. On a hunch, he rose, took a chair, and propped it beneath the doorknob. Pulling another chair close to the bed, he hung the Peacemaker and holster on it and, climbing into bed again, settled in. He soon dozed off.

A light sleeper, the sound of a key being fitted into the door's lock and the tweak of the lock turning brought Walt awake. The knob twisted, but the chair beneath the knob kept the door closed. Reaching for the Peacemaker, Walt slipped from the bed. The murkiness of the room relieved somewhat by the dim light from the window enabled him to move quickly across the room just as something slammed against the door, smashing the chair to splinters, and flinging the door open. An instant later, successive blasts from a shotgun jarred the bed, showering the room with feathers from the pillows where Walt's head had rested moments before.

Walt risked a shot as the man turned and ran, but missed. The shooter was at the end of the hall by the time he made the door, but he sent two more quick shots after him, missing again. When he reached the lobby, wearing nothing but his underwear, the clerk was peering fearfully over the desk.

"Did you know him?" Walt demanded.

"No, sir!"

"Have you ever seen him before?"

"I don't know, sir."

"What do you mean you don't know?"

"He was wearing a mask, sir!"

Walking to the hotel entryway, Walt stepped out onto the boardwalk. The street was dark and, as far as he could see, nothing moved in either direction. Nor was there any sound, and Walt noted that even the saloons had closed. Returning to the desk, he asked the clerk for another room and was given a key to the room next to the one he had occupied. When he climbed the stairs, occupants stood before open doors. The few women did not seem too embarrassed to see Walt in his underwear.

"What happened?" a man asked.

"Intruders," Walt replied. "Broke into my room," he added, indicating the smashed door.

He glanced at Misty's door, which remained closed. Stopping before it, he knocked, but there was no answer. Wondering where she could be, he transferred his belongings to the new room. Only after he had settled in did it occur to him that Misty Wells might have told her uncle where he was. Could that explain why she hadn't answered his knock? Or maybe she had already left the hotel.

Ruby Barry stood on the front porch of the two–room, shotgun house she rented, given that name because one could stand before the house and shoot a gun through both rooms without hitting anything, a style made popular in frontier Texas. "What's that money for?" she asked a second time.

"It's just a gift freely given with no strings, Mrs. Barry," Richard Courtney said. "Someone instructed me to give it to you."

"Who would want to give me so much money, and want nothing in return?" the widow asked, still suspicious.

"I can't tell you that, Mrs. Barry," Courtney said. "I've been forbidden to tell by the gentleman who is making the gift."

"And he expects nothing in return?" Ruby Barry asked again unbelievingly.

"Nothing. Absolutely nothing," Courtney insisted.

Maudie Barry stood just behind her mother. "Take the money, Ma," she said. "Think what we can do with a thousand dollars."

"What would you do with it?" Ruby Barry asked her daughter.

"First, I'd buy me some nice clothes. Then I'd go live in Denver."

"A thousand dollars wouldn't last forever," Ruby Barry said. "What would you do when it ran out?"

"I . . . I don't know, Ma, but a thousand dollars would last a long time."

Ruby Barry studied Courtney for another moment or so. "You sure there're no strings attached?" she asked again.

"Absolutely none," repeated Courtney.

"Then I'll take it," she said and accepted the money.

"Mind if I ask how you intend to spend it?" asked Courtney.

"Don't mind at all," she said and, turning to her daughter, gave her fifty dollars. "Spend that anyway you want," she said, "but when it's gone, there won't be any more in a lump sum, just enough to take care of your real needs.

"I'll take some and buy us a bigger home," she said to Courtney, "so we can have a room to ourselves. With some of what's left, I'll turn this place into a laundry. There is a Chinese family I know who I'll hire to help out. But I'll manage everything myself to make sure my customers are satisfied."

"Sounds like a good plan," Richard Courtney said, pleased. "I guess your benefactor knew what he was doing."

"You won't tell me who he is so I can thank him?" she asked a final time.

"He forbids it," Courtney replied.

Chapter Eight

After breakfast at the hotel dining room, Walt stopped by the desk as the night clerk was being relieved. "What time did Miss Wells check out last night?" he asked.

The clerk studied the register a moment, then turned and looked at the key board. "I have no record of her checking out," he said, "and she hasn't turned in her key. Are you sure she's not still in her room?"

"Pretty sure," Walt replied. "I knocked but got no answer. Do you have an extra key?"

"Certainly."

"Then maybe you should check the room," Walt suggested.

Passing on through the lobby, Walt stepped out on the boardwalk. Before continuing on the errand he had in mind, he studied the busy street, wondering if Wells might have set up an ambush. Seeing no suspicious looking characters lingering about, he continued on, keeping a close watch until he came to The Prentiss Herald, the local newspaper.

"What can I do for you, sir?" asked a clerk at the front counter.

"I'd like to place an advertisement," replied Walt.

The clerk, a towheaded young man barely old enough to shave, gave him a form. "If you'll fill this out," he said, passing Walt a slip of paper.

Walt wrote:

Wanted: honest men who can shoot and are not afraid to face danger. Pay appropriate. Inquire at room 27 Prentiss Hotel.

"How much?" he asked, returning the paper to the clerk.

The clerk counted the words. "That'll be thirty-five cents."

"When will it appear?" asked Walt, paying the man.

The clerk glanced at his watch. "You got here just in time for this afternoon's paper which will be on the street by about three o'clock."

Walt's next stop was the land office. The man who rose from his desk to greet him wore black pants, matching vest, and a stiff-collared white shirt with a black string bowtie. He had a scrawny neck, a shiny bald pate, and pale blue eyes whose twinkle managed to soften the over-all scholarly impression.

"Sam Stoner," he introduced himself. "I'm the land agent." He extended his hand.

"Walt Davis," replied Walt. They shook, the agent's hand dry but firm.

"Now, how can I help you?" the agent asked.

"I'd like to file on a piece of land if it's not already taken," Walt replied.

"Follow me," Stoner said and led Walt to a large map of Colorado hanging on a wall in the rear of the office. "Now point out this piece of land to me," the agent said.

"Here," and Walt put his finger on the land his father had once claimed.

Stoner led the way to a table on which lay two binders, each several inches thick. He pulled one to him and flipped through the pages until he found what he wanted. He studied the page a moment and turned to Walt.

"Sorry. That land is already taken," he said.

"Can you tell me who filed on it?" asked Walt.

"Strange," the agent said. "The name on the papers is Angus Davis." The agent looked at Walt. "Any relation?" he asked.

"My father," Walt said.

"Tell you what," Stoner said. "The back taxes are more than the land is worth. You pay those and the place is yours. That way I won't need any proof of who you are."

Walt's excitement was so great he could hardly keep his hands steady as he counted out the money and passed it over to Sam Stoner.

"Take a few days to get you the paperwork," Stoner said as he wrote out a receipt.

"I'll check with you the next time I'm in town," Walt said. "Meanwhile, I reckon it's okay if I settle on the land?"

"Certainly," Stoner said, "the land is yours." He made a note to himself on a piece of paper on his desk.

Walt hadn't felt so good for years. He'd settle on his own land and wait for Evan Wells to try and move him off. If Wells won, so be it, but Walt would be defending himself and his property if a fight developed. If Wells, or any of his men, were killed in such a fight, no lawman in Colorado would call it murder.

"What did you find out about Miss Wells?" Walt asked the clerk when he returned to the hotel.

"The room was empty, and her things were gone," said

the clerk. "I guess she left sometime during the night without me seeing her."

Maybe while you were asleep, Walt thought, but kept it to himself. "I'll be having some callers this afternoon," Walt said. "They'll not know my name, but they'll be inquiring about work. Send them up to my room one at a time. Is that too much to ask?"

"No, sir," replied the clerk.

"Then take this for your trouble," Walt said and tossed the man a five dollar gold piece.

"Thank you, sir!" the clerk replied, catching the coin, and glancing from the coin to Walt's retreating back.

Surprising the services a little money can buy, Walt thought to himself. *Evan Wells may never realize the power he's accidentally placed in my hands by chasing me into the mountains.*

Chapter Nine

The first applicant came a little after four o'clock, an hour after the newspaper hit the streets. Walt, answering the knock, crossed to the door and opened it.

"You the fella looking for help?" a man asked.

"I'm the man," Walt replied.

The caller's broad shoulders stretched a faded blue work shirt tight. The six-foot frame was lean and fit, the face a leather brown from years in the sun. "I'm Kell Franklin," he said. "My friends call me Kell. I came about the ad in the paper." He removed his Stetson, exposing dark hair with gray edging the temples. Gray–green eyes assessed Walt carefully. Walt guessed his age to be in the mid–thirties.

"Walt Davis." They shook. "Come in and have a seat, Mr. Franklin," Walt said. He led the man into the room and indicated a chair he'd placed near the window. "First, I'd like to know something about you," Walt said, taking the other chair.

Kell Franklin crossed to the chair and sat. "Well, let me see," he began. "I've worked on ranches off and on from

60

Texas to Montana. I was a deputy marshal for a time in San Antonio, and I spent a year in jail in Abilene."

That Franklin would confess such a thing right off impressed Walt. "What for?" he asked.

"I hit a saloon after a long cattle drive. I got roaring drunk and got into a brawl. By then I was both drunk and broke, and I smashed the place up some. When I didn't have the money to pay for the damage, the judge gave me six months."

"Didn't you have any friends to help out with the money?"

"Oh, I had some friends, but by then they were as broke as I was."

"How about the man you worked for?"

"He was a penny pincher. Wouldn't lend me a dime."

"You said you were once a lawman. Why did you give up the law?" Walt asked.

"I didn't like the pay and being a target for drunks."

"Do you have a job now?"

"No, but I been promised a riding job if I want to take it. I decided I'd like to find out what kind of work you're offering. Let me say up front, I never took money to kill a man, and I don't intend to start now."

"I need some good men to help me defend my place against intruders who might try to run me off," Walt replied. "There might be killing, but I'll never ask you to break the law. Now, could I have a look at your six–gun?"

"What for?" Kell Franklin asked a little nervously.

"A man's gun and his gear tell a lot about a man," Walt replied.

Kell Franklin hesitated a moment, and then drew a Colt .45 from its holster and gave the gun to Walt butt first. The gun was about what Walt expected. It had a well used, well kept look. Bone handles were worn smooth. The metal was well polished, with no flecks of rust or signs of ill use.

"Well kept," Walt said, returning the gun.

He studied Kell Franklin a moment longer. The man seemed honest and dependable and Walt, knowing he was in a position to change his mind at any time, made his decision. "I'll pay you a hundred a month and food; and after me, you'll be in charge," he said. "Is that satisfactory?"

"I have another question myself," Kell Franklin said.

"Yes."

"Who will we likely be fighting?"

"Evan Wells," Walt replied. He waited a moment and then asked, "You still interested in the job?"

"Brock Thurston, Wells' foreman, is the man who offered me the riding job."

"Then maybe you're not interested." Walt said.

"I'm your man, Mr. Davis."

"Call me Walt."

"On one condition."

"What's that?"

"You call me Kell."

"You got a deal, Kell," and the two men stood and shook again.

Walt gave him twenty dollars. "An advance," he said, "just in case. Take a room here at the hotel, and let me know which one. When I decide on the next man, I'll send him along to you. You decide if he's a man you can work with. If not, let him go."

Walt interviewed numerous men the rest of that afternoon, that evening, and the following morning, selecting two more who struck him as the kind of men he wanted. One was a man in his late twenties, Phillip Boyd. He was dressed like the farmer he had lately been. He weighed around two hundred pounds and wore brown corduroy pants, a faded red shirt, a narrow-brimmed straw hat, and dusty, scratched boots. Intense green eyes with an angry cast dominated a sunburned face. He looked anything but a gunman, but Walt sized him up to be honest and a fighter once his loyalty was earned.

"Anything troubling you, Boyd?" Walt asked after studying the man a moment.

"The same thing happened to me that happened to your pa."

"How do you know what happened to my father?"

"People talk. I listen."

"I won't have your personal revenge interfering with my plans," Walt said.

"I can hold off on my revenge, Mr. Davis, because I believe that sooner or later you'll pay Evan Wells in full for the evil he's done to your pa and others."

"Are you sure you can control your anger?" asked Walt.

"I'll lay my hand on the Bible and swear it," replied Boyd.

"Your word is good enough for me," Walt said.

"You have it, sir."

"I'd like the men in this outfit to be on a first name basis. Call me Walt. I'll call you Phillip."

"Other folks call me Phil if that's all right with you."

"You haven't asked me specifically about what you'll be involved in," Walt said.

"I figure you'll let me know when you're ready," replied Boyd, an answer which pleased Walt.

The other was Jim Chaney, who was about twenty and the youngest of the three. He was a youngster Walt had known in Kansas and liked.

Kell Franklin had approved of Phillip Boyd and Jim Chaney, and the following morning, Walt met with his crew in his hotel room. "Time I let you in on my plans," he told them. "When I'm finished, if anyone wants out, he has only to tell me. There'll be no hard feelings."

An expectant silence met Walt's announcement.

"As you may know, Evan Wells hanged my father and ran my mother and me off our ranch some years back," Walt began. "I've recently paid the back taxes, and the land now belongs to me. I intend to reoccupy my ranch and build a home there. I expect Evan Wells will try to run me off again. I don't intend to let him. That probably means a fight, but everything we do will be legal. I'll fire any man who does anything to break the law and turn him over to the sheriff in Denver City myself. Any man who can't accept that should get up and leave now."

No one moved.

"All right," Walt said, looking pleased.

"Now, does anyone know where my place is?"

Phillip Boyd lifted a hand. "I've been by there."

"Good. You show Jim the way and wait till I arrive. Kell and I'll be along in a day or so. I expect Wells has already guessed my intentions, so keep alert, especially at night."

"You can depend on us, Walt," Boyd replied. The fervor in his voice suggested he looked forward to any clash with Evan Wells or his men.

"Mr. Davis . . . Walt," Phil Boyd said and stood. "You didn't ask and I didn't tell you, but I'm married. Is there any chance I could take my wife along? If you don't have a cook, she's a mighty fine one."

"I don't have a cook, Phil, but this is apt to get dangerous. You better leave Mrs. Boyd here in Prentiss. I'll give you a day off now and then to ride in and see her."

"I mentioned as much to her, but Connie says she's willing to face a few bullets and refuses to stay behind." Phil Boyd said. "Would you talk to her? Maybe she'll listen to you."

The idea of trying to persuade another man's wife to do anything was an unpleasant sounding chore, and Walt wanted nothing to do with it. "Well, if she knows what we're in for, I reckon you can bring her along," he said after a moment. "If she's willing to cook, I'll pay her a cook's wages, but make sure she knows I don't think bringing her is a good idea."

"I'll make sure," replied Phil Boyd, looking as if he'd just been saved from execution.

"Can she ride?" asked Walt.

"She can ride, but I got a small wagon," Phil said. "We'll load our things in that, and she can drive the team."

"Tell her that from today on, she's on the payroll, and tell her to shop for supplies and bring them with her in the wagon." Walt passed Phil a couple of large bills. "Tell her to buy quality. And tell her also to be ready to cook a meal or two along the way, since your wagon will slow us up a bit."

"Yes, sir," Phil said and left hurriedly, seemingly afraid Walt might change his mind.

Chapter Ten

"What're we staying in town for?" Kell asked when the others were gone.

"First, we're going to need more money than I've got on me, so we'll stop by the bank. Then you'll buy what's on this list, starting with a wagon and four mules to pull it."

Kell glanced at the list. "What're we gonna build? A fort?" he asked. "One wagon might not haul all this."

"Then buy two," Walt replied. "We'll be cutting and hauling logs, and a second wagon would come in handy if the first were to break down."

When they entered the bank, Richard Courtney rushed to meet them. "Good to see you, Mr. Davis!" he exclaimed, pumping Walt's hand. "What can we do for you today?"

"I'm buying some building materials," Walt replied. "I figure a couple thousand ought to do it."

"Houston, bring Mr. Davis two thousand dollars!" Courtney took Walt's arm and led him to one of the chairs before his desk. Kell followed, an amused look on his face at the banker's desire to please.

"I have some interesting news for you," Courtney said when all three men were seated.

"What's that?" asked Walt.

"I think you'll be impressed with the way your gift is being spent," Courtney replied. "Mrs. Barry has bought a larger house for her and her daughter and turned her old home into a laundry. She's hired a Chinese family to work for her, but she's to manage the business herself."

"Sounds like a very sensible plan," Walt said.

Houston, the clerk, arrived with the money. Walt signed for it and, rising, tucked the bills in his pocket.

"Anything else?" Courtney asked. "Anything at all?"

"No, sir," replied Walt, "and I want to thank you for services already rendered, and I might be asking more favors from you in the future."

"As I said, anything at all, sir," Courtney replied.

"Come along, Kell," Walt said to his foreman. "We got some serious buying to do."

By the time they were finished, the day was rushing toward an end. "Why don't we travel for a couple hours and find a place to camp and spend the night," Walt suggested.

"Suits me," Kell agreed, and each tied their mount behind one of the wagons, climbed aboard, and set out.

There were only a couple of springs between Prentiss and the ranch and one, Walt recalled, was a place where he had camped a few times with his father and mother on the long trips into town. *We should be able to make it there by sundown,* he thought to himself and slapped the lines against the backs of the mules, asking for a little more speed.

The site was more refreshing than Walt remembered. A small stream cascaded over a low bluff and gathered in clear pools of emerald–green water in the bottom of a shallow arroyo. He recalled the cave that could barely be seen behind the thin sheet of falling water that fed the tall grass growing along the runoff. A few willows, hawthorns, and a spruce or two had grown up along the stream, complementing the usual cottonwoods.

"Nice spot," Kell said when Walt pulled up. Kell pulled his wagon alongside Walt's and climbed down. "Nice timing too. Be sundown shortly."

"I camped here a few times with my folks when I was a kid," Walt said.

"Guess it holds some memories for you then," Kell replied.

"Some. You take care of the mules and horses, and I'll rustle up some food," Walt suggested.

"You bet," Kell replied and, stepping down, got busy.

By the time Kell had staked out the animals and returned, Walt had coffee boiling beside a fire and was slicing bacon into a frying pan. When the bacon was crisp, he took it up and sliced potatoes into the hot grease.

"How about a cup of coffee while the potatoes cook?" he asked.

"I'll pour," Kell said and reached for the cups Walt had set aside.

They sat on their haunches, backs to trees, the smell of sizzling bacon permeating the place. A couple of camp robbers settled onto the lower limbs of a nearby cottonwood and eyed the camp, waiting for scraps. Nearby an insect chirped his night song a little early.

"Noticed you looking to the rear a few times," Kell said. "You expecting trouble?"

"Nothing would surprise me," Walt replied. "Evan Wells has his ways of knowing what's going on, and he's an impatient man. He won't waste time coming after me."

"Us," Kell said.

"Us then," replied Walt, "and it's good to hear you say it. You want the first watch or the first sleep?"

"I'll take the first watch," Kell replied.

They tossed a few scraps to the camp robbers and scoured the frypan and dishes at the spring. Kell rolled a smoke. He lit the cigarette with a small burning twig from the fast dying fire. "You better turn in," he said after a couple of deep draws on the smoke. "I'll be shaking you awake before you know it."

"What time is it?" Walt asked when Kell shook him awake.

"About two."

"You should have waked me earlier." Walt pushed himself up and stretched.

"Here, this will help," Kell said and gave him a cup of hot coffee.

Walt took a sip. "Texas coffee," he said and smiled.

"You know about Texas coffee?" asked Kell.

"Thick enough to float a horseshoe," Walt replied and chuckled.

"Been boiling for awhile, I reckon," Kell said.

Walt piled a couple of limbs on the fire as Kell climbed into his bedroll. Kell had rolled a stone in near the fire and, coffee cup in hand, Walt sat and listened to Kell's instant snores. The trees around him were bigger and taller now than when he was a boy, but the spring was the same. He recalled one occasion when he and his folks had camped here. He couldn't have been over five or six, and he saw in his mind his mother spreading his blankets and tucking him in. Then Christina and Angus had sat beside the fire and held hands as they talked of what they would do when the ranch was turning a profit. The memory was so fresh in his mind that Walt could still recall the murmur of their voices.

The attack came a little before dawn. Enough light prevailed that Walt happened to see the heads of the mules lift from their grazing and stare in the direction of Prentiss. He rose from his position beside the fire and followed the mules' gaze. He saw nothing and turned back. At the same instant a bullet slammed into the cottonwood before which he'd been standing.

Throwing himself to the ground, Walt grabbed his rifle and, crawling to where Kell lay, shook his shoulder roughly,

"They're here!" he urgently whispered, to his foreman.

Kell was already awake and reaching for his six-gun. He crawled after Walt into the trees surrounding the spring as another bullet pounded into a limb above their heads.

"The sucker don't shoot too well," Kell whispered as both men sent bullets at the shooter's gun flash, apparently missing. That response brought a fusillade of bullets from various directions. "My God, how many are out there?"

"Enough to keep us busy," replied Walt as more shots sounded, some closer in.

"Shoot when you see anything, but keep your head down," Walt said as he pushed himself backward toward the wagons. Climbing up the front wheel of the one he had driven, he reached beneath the seat and brought up a package of dynamite he'd bought for blowing up stumps. Quickly, he separated two sticks of dynamite and spliced them with six inches of detonator cord. Making sure he had matches in his pocket, he returned to where Kell lay.

"Take one of these," he said, and handed Kell one of the sticks. "Keep firing at the bastards, but stay low," he instructed. "When they're within throwing distance, you toss your stick slightly to the right. I'll do the same to the left. Maybe we'll kill some of them, but those that turn and run will make good targets."

"You think of everything," Kell said and chuckled.

The circle was closing, but more cautiously as the attackers got nearer, obviously slowed by the accuracy of the returning fire. In the east the rim of the sun appeared, peeping over the horizon like the edge of a great red eye.

"Who you reckon they are?" asked Kell.

"Got to be Wells' men," replied Walt. "He's the only one I got a fight with that I know of."

"My rifle is empty," Kell said after a shot. "Keep 'em busy while I reload."

"Don't think you'll have time," Walt said. "Here they come! Light your dynamite!"

Both men dropped their rifles and, hugging the ground, struck matches and held the flames to the detonator cords. They made sure the cords were well lit and then, coming to their knees, tossed the dynamite almost simultaneously.

"Dynamite!" someone yelled as the sparkling sticks sailed through the air and hit, followed by almost concurrent explosions.

Screams of pain followed the blasts as men here and there turned tail and ran, attempting to flee even faster when they heard the rifles exploding behind them. They vanished in the gloom, and all that remained were two craters where the dynamite had landed and a spreading cloud of dust drifting off to the east, turned pink by the first rays of the sun.

"Let's get out of here before they decide to come back," Walt said.

"Doubtful they'll try that," replied Kell, "after the beating they just took. How many you reckon we got?"

"Not enough," Walt replied, but he counted three bodies when Kell went to bring the mules in. Ten minutes later they pulled out, heading in the direction of the ranch.

"Pretty fancy idea, that dynamite!" Kell yelled from well back of Walt. "That should give Wells' boys something to think about!"

"This fight has just begun!" Walt called back. "Wells is as stubborn as a sullen ox! Losing two or three men will only make him madder."

Chapter Eleven

"Whoa there!" Walt called to the mules and pulled them up in the shade of the cottonwood. Kell parked his wagon nearby. The sun was straight overhead and, as both men climbed down over a front wheel, Phil Boyd and Jim Chaney came to meet them.

"Been keeping an eye out for you all morning," Phil said.

"You have any trouble here?" Walt asked.

"Quiet as a mouse," Boyd replied.

"Something smells mighty good," Kell observed.

"Connie has kept the stew hot just in case," Phil said. "Come along. I expect she's got a couple of bowls filled already."

"You want these wagons unloaded and the teams unhitched, Walt?" Jim Chaney asked.

"You bet!" Walt called back over his shoulder. "You'll find a couple of tents in my wagon. Unload them and begin stringing them up. Kell and I'll help out as soon as we've put away some of this stew."

The stew was delicious, and Connie Boyd bustled about

keeping coffee cups filled, fresh baked bread handy, and replenishing the stew when a bowl was emptied.

"That was as good as I've ever eaten, Mrs. Boyd," Walt said, setting his bowl aside.

Connie Boyd turned to face Walt. As she wiped her hands on her apron, she gave Walt a severe look. "You call me Connie from now on," she said. "or the stew may not be so good next time."

"Connie it is from here on," Walt said and laughed.

By the time Walt and Kell returned to the wagons, Phil and Jim had the two tents strung out and ready to put up. "We'll need some poles," Kell said and glanced up the slope down which the stream ran. "Looks to be plenty up there," he said. "Grab a couple of axes and follow me, men," he said and led the way up the slope.

"Store all the food supplies and house things in the smaller tent," Walt instructed the men when the tents were up. "Phil and Connie will sleep in that tent. Store anything else that'll need to be under a shelter in case of rain in the big tent. The rest of us will spread our bedrolls in there. Kell, you take charge. I think I'll climb up the hill and have a look around."

As the men fell to, Walt made his way up the slope. When he reached the spring, he saw a boulder he'd perched on many times as a boy. Sitting down on a large stone, the years seemed to slip away, and Walt, gazing back down to where his men worked, saw himself as a boy playing happily in the shade of the cottonwood. Then, in his mind's eye, he saw the men pull up before the cabin, saw his father emerge, and a man toss a loop about his father's shoulders, dragging Angus Davis to the cottonwood and throwing the rope over a limb. He saw again Evan Wells slap the horse on which they'd placed his father, saw his father begin to struggle and swing, felt again the deep pangs of grief and anger all over again at his father's cruel murder.

Turning back to the camp, Walt noticed for the first time that Connie Boyd had chosen almost the same spot to put her cooking fire as Christina Davis had chosen during that long ago time and, instead of Connie, Walt suddenly saw his mother stooping over to stir the hot, steaming pot.

Walt hadn't wept in years, but the vision brought moisture to his eyes, and he thought of the difference in Christina Davis then and as she had been at her death, a mere scrap of the woman he and his father had once loved and cherished. He shook his head to blot out the haunting vision and focused his eyes on the rolling plains that stretched toward Prentiss. In the distance, the wind stirred up a dust devil that, in turn, sucked up bits of debris and spat it out through the top of the funnel, leaving fragments of earth's rubble trailing in the air behind the twirling dust. Lowering himself over the little pool surrounding the spring, he drank deeply of the cool water and, refreshed, made his way down the slope to join in the work.

When the tents were up and all the gear and supplies stowed away, Walt collected the men around him. He drew a rough map of the area, identifying the cottonwood, the tents, and the stream. "I want thigh-deep pits dug here, here, and here," he told the group. "Pile a bulwark of stones before each pit for a breastwork. The pits won't be manned until there is need. However, during daylight hours a guard will be posted at all times up there by the spring where there's a good view of the surrounding country. If there's any sign at all that someone is approaching, he'll fire two shots into the air. That'll be the signal to leave whatever you're doing and man one of the pits. At night the guard will take up a position down here near the tents and keep his eyes and ears open.

"I've already told you what we're up against, and you know of the attack on Kell and me the other day. The dynamite saved us, but they may come with dynamite themselves next time, so be alert for anything out of the ordinary. Our lives will depend on our vigilance. Keep that in mind. Any questions?" Walt asked, looking at each of the men in turn.

There were none.

"Kell, you work up a schedule and include me." Walt glanced at the sun, which was a couple of hours above the western horizon. "We'll take the rest of the day off from regular work, but I'd like every man to see that both his six-guns and his rifles are cleaned, oiled, and in good working order. You may have noticed the crate of Winchesters I bought. There's also a dozen Colt .45s in another box. If anyone's guns are not in good working order, take one of those. Might be a good idea if everyone got both a second rifle and six-gun oiled and in good working order, just in case. Kell, you check their guns and see that each man has a bullet belt full of cartridges."

Chapter Twelve

Ezra Dudley, the cook, glared at Misty as she entered the kitchen.

"You're late!" the old cook snapped and dredged up a half–hearted glare.

"I know, Ezra," Misty said. "I couldn't bring myself to hurry. Will you forgive me?"

The cook dredged up a second stare even less energized and brought a plate of food from the stove. Elderly and grizzled, Ezra Dudley stood a little above five feet. He wore a beard to compensate for a pate as smooth as a door knob. His skin color resembled the dough he kneaded into biscuits for each meal. He had been with the W–in–a–Box for more years than Misty had been alive.

"I won't feed you next time you come down so late," he grumbled as he placed the plate of bacon and eggs and a cup of coffee on the table before Misty. "Eat," he said, "and I hope everything's cold."

"You're just an old sweetheart, Ezra," Misty said and reached a hand out to the old man's arm. "But where is everyone?" she asked, beginning to eat.

"Your uncle is in his study," Ezra told her. "The punchers are rounding up strays near the foothills."

The expression on the old cook's face remained sour, but his eyes were warm as he returned to the stove and poured himself a cup of coffee. With cup in hand, he came back to the table and sat across from Misty. "What're your plans for the day?" he asked.

"Thought I'd take a ride," replied Misty. "Looked like a nice day when I peeked out my window."

"Want me to wrap something for your lunch?" the old man asked.

"I might get hungry before I get back. A sandwich would be nice."

"Sounds like you intend to ride a long way," the cook said. He went to the table beside the stove and made a sandwich of ham and bread, wrapped it, and brought it to the table.

"I thought I might pay our neighbor a visit," Misty said.

"Walt Davis?"

"Yes."

"Better not let your uncle catch you visiting that man," the cook said. "They're worst enemies, and one thing your uncle insists on is loyalty. Ain't no telling what he'd do if he caught you, so be careful."

"I'm not afraid of him," Misty replied. "I'm not a minor, and he has no authority over me. I'm free to do as I want. What would you say if I told you I've been thinking of moving into Prentiss?"

The idea turned the old cook thoughtful. "Mr. Wells would never agree to that," said the cook after a moment. "He'd cut you off without a penny."

"I don't need his money. I've got the money from my father's place back in Virginia. Enough to last me a long time if I'm careful."

"But why would you want to leave?" asked Ezra, attempting to hide his disappointment.

"I don't like some of the things I hear Uncle Evan has done," Misty replied. "There are rumors that he's run people off their property, even killed some. I don't like being a part of anything like that."

"But even if it's true, you have nothing to do with it."

"I get some of the association if I live here and live off Uncle Evan's bounty," Misty insisted.

"I reckon I get your meaning," replied Ezra.

"Thanks for breakfast."

Rising and reaching for the sandwich, Misty took a lump of sugar from the bowl. As she retraced her steps through the house, she heard her uncle's voice coming from the study. Afraid he might hear her, she tiptoed through the hallway, found her hat, and stepped outside. The last thing she needed at the moment was a confrontation with her uncle. That would come when she told him she was moving out.

That day, as she had seen through her window, had turned out fine, and not so warm as to be too uncomfortable. A slight breeze drifted down from the mountains and chased a few fleecy clouds along the peaks.

The palomino saw her and whinnied a welcome from the barn. Misty smiled and crossed the yard to the corral. She gave the pony the sugar, got his headgear, slipped it on, and led him outside to the tack room. She brushed his blond back smooth, spread the saddle blanket, making sure there were no wrinkles, and lifted the saddle to his back. She saw the pony's belly swell as she tightened the cinch. Smiling, she slapped him there, and he relaxed as he always did as Misty drew the cinch tight.

"You'll learn sometime you can't fool me like that," she said and patted the pony's neck affectionately.

Climbing into the saddle, she turned him north on a route parallel to the blue outline of the Rockies in the distance.

Her thoughts returned to the conversation with Ezra. She liked the idea of moving into town, liked the idea of being independent. As long as she lived on the W–in–a–Box, she would be indebted to her uncle, whether she approved of what he did or not. She'd begin packing when she returned from the ride.

The morning matched Misty's suddenly brighter mood. The sun gave the steep slopes of the Rockies a gentler look, but, rough or gentle, she loved the mountains. There was something mysterious but promising when one stared into their depths. She had spent some time exploring the foothills during spring and summer when the weather was nice, and she recognized the various shades of green produced by different trees—the pale green of the aspen, the blue green of the spruce, the darker green of the pine and fir.

She imagined the sunny meadows that would be filled with colorful columbine, sunflower, and Indian paintbrush, not to mention the raspberries, thimbleberries, and wild mountain blueberries—the favorite foods of bears.

After a nice ride, if a little long, Misty topped the last rise and pulled up, surprised. Instead of the half–deserted site she expected, she saw a tent camp bustling with activity. As two shots rang out from the hill behind the camp, the men dropped what they were doing and scrambled into pits behind breastworks. Misty had no idea what to make of such activity. She sent the pony down the slope, knowing she would be recognized as a woman, and no man would dare fire a shot at her. A moment later, Walt Davis stepped from a tent and came to meet her.

"That was a bit dangerous, Miss Wells, riding up on us like that," he said and lifted a hand to help her from the saddle. "We've been expecting an attack from your uncle."

Misty looked around at the camp as men crawled from the pits and began whatever they had been doing before her appearance. "You seem well prepared for when he does," she said, "but you know he could hit you with twenty men if he chooses, and I expect he will. He can't afford to lose this fight with you. Every man he's ever wronged would rise up against him."

"That's part of the idea," Walt replied, "but I'd rather not talk about that. Can I offer you a cup of coffee?"

"Coffee would be nice."

"That's the cook tent," Walt said and preceded her inside. "Connie, this is Miss Wells," he said, introducing Misty to Connie Phillips.

"Miss Wells," Connie replied, acknowledging the introduction.

"Nice to meet you, Connie. Please call me Misty."

"Certainly, and thank you."

"We thought you might give us a cup of coffee," Walt said.

"I just made a fresh pot." Connie moved briskly to the stove on the far side of the tent.

Walt pulled a chair out from the long plank and saw-horse table. "This is a little rough," he said, "but it's the best I can offer right now. Maybe you'll visit again when we have better accommodations."

Misty sat, but didn't reply.

Connie brought their coffee amid the crackle of wood burning in the stove and the whistle of a steam kettle. From beyond the tent came the sound of someone chopping wood. Someone must have told a joke, because Misty heard loud laughter.

"Is it worth risking the lives of the men out there just

to make a point with Uncle Evan?" Misty asked, her eyes meeting Walt's across the top of the cup she was holding.

"It's more than that," Walt replied. "My father bought and paid for this land. I found out from Sam Stoner in the land office that the land was still in his name. I paid the back taxes, and it belongs to me now. This is my home. If I leave it, I'll leave feet first, the way my father did. That's how important it is to me."

"Men are so full of pride," Misty said. "You and Uncle Evan are a lot alike in that respect. No amount of land is worth the lives of men. And I'm told you seem to have lots of money now, Walt. Why risk it all to fight a battle you're apt to lose and maybe get yourself and your men killed in the process?"

"Why do you assume I'll lose?" Walt asked.

Misty was silent for a moment, her expression thoughtful. "I've learned something about you," she said. "You've got scruples. Uncle Evan has none. That puts you at a disadvantage."

Walt was pleasantly surprised that she'd gone to the trouble to make inquiries about him, if that was what she meant. But why would a girl like Misty Wells be interested in him?

"It's more than just pride with me, Misty," he said after a moment. "I owe something to the memory of my father. Evan Wells hanged my father from the limb of that cottonwood out there. I heard and saw him give the order. A day never passes that I don't see his man lassoing my father, dropping a noose over his head, and your uncle slapping the horse he was on. I intend to make Evan Wells suffer and pay for that murder, and everyone else who helped with it."

"You think killing Uncle Evan will wipe out that terrible act?"

"I didn't say I intended to kill him, but before I'm finished, I'll see him stripped of his lands and wealth. I want him to experience what he's put other men through."

Misty rose. "I suppose I knew before I said anything how you'd react. I don't guess I can blame you. I just wish it could be different."

"You're leaving?" Walt asked.

"Yes. I have to get back and start packing. I'm moving into town tomorrow."

"I'll ride with you part of the way," Walt said. "When did you decide to move into town?" he asked after a few minutes.

"I've been thinking of it for a long time," she replied, "but I just decided to move this morning."

Outside, he helped Misty into the saddle and climbed astride Cougar. "I'll be back in a little while," he said to Kell who stood nearby.

"No need to hurry," Kell said, smiling. "Have a nice ride."

"Where did you disappear to that night in the hotel?" Walt asked after they had ridden a few minutes.

"I slipped out and found Uncle Evan," replied Misty. "I told him I was sick and needed to return to the ranch."

"I guess it worked," Walt said.

"I didn't want the two of you running into each other. I told you I was afraid of what might happen."

"But somebody told him," Walt said.

"I know, but I don't know who it was."

Walt had no response, and they rode together in silence for another mile or so. "Guess I better turn back here," Walt said and pulled up.

"Thank you for the escort," Misty said and smiled. "Good luck with your ranch."

"If things were different, I'd like to call on you, Misty," Walt said, surprising himself.

She stared at him for a long moment. Then, without

speaking, touched the pony's sides with her heels, urging him into a quick gallop. After a moment, she turned back and waved.

Walt stared after her until she was out of sight and then watched the up-tailing of her dust for a moment before turning around.

Chapter Thirteen

They kept a constant watch for several weeks, but the anticipated attack didn't come. Meanwhile, the building went well, first the cabin, then a bunkhouse and, finally, a small cabin in the back for Phil and Connie Boyd. They had commenced building the corral when they began to run short of nails.

"Someone's got to ride into Prentiss for nails," Kell observed to Walt before they began work next morning.

"Let me go!" young Jim Chaney volunteered. "I ain't been to town in a coon's age."

"Too dangerous," Walt replied. "You might run into some of the W–in–a–Box crew. I don't want you having trouble with them."

"Aw, Walt!" the youngster grumbled. "You worry too much. I'll stop in and have one beer, get the nails, and ride back. Won't none of Wells' crew be in town this early. I'll be back here before you know it."

The look on Jim's face was so hopeful and eager that Walt couldn't refuse. "You make sure you are," Walt replied, giving in reluctantly.

Jim gave a whoop and raced for the corral, quickly

roped his bay, and saddled up. Climbing into the saddle, he stopped by the spot where Walt and Kell were working. "You forgot to give me any money," he said to Walt.

"You didn't give me time," Walt said and laughed. Taking a bill from the roll in his pocket, he gave it to Jim. "There'll be enough left over to pay for that beer," he said.

"And pick me up a couple of sacks of tobacco," Kell said.

"See you later!" the youngster called as he rode off.

Jim Chaney's first stop was the blacksmith shop where Andy Tew held sway. The sleeves of Tew's sweat–stained shirt were cut off at his shoulders. His arms and hands were dark from soot and smoke and rippled with muscle when they moved. He wore soot–stained boots, khaki pants, and a dirty leather cap pulled low over his eyes. A leather apron was tied about his waist.

"What can I do for you, younker?" he asked as Jim entered the shop.

"Walt sent me in for some nails," Jim said.

"What size?" asked Tew.

"That size should be about right," Jim said, indicating a bin of nails near the anvil.

"Just finished hammering those out yesterday," replied Tew. "How many pounds?"

"Ten," replied Jim, and watched Andy Tew scoop the nails onto a nearby scale.

"There," Tew said, as he placed a final scoop of nails on the scales, "and a half scoop for good measure." He emptied the nails into a small flour sack. "What're you fellas working on?"

"House, barn, toilet; you name it, and we've built it," replied Jim.

"I ain't taking sides in this fight," Tew said as he followed Jim outside to his horse. He looked carefully in all directions before he continued, "but you tell Walt to be careful. There's been talk."

"Who's been talking and what've they been saying?" asked Jim. He swung into the saddle and looked down at Andy Tew.

"Some of Wells' men were in town last night," Tew said. "They were saying Walt and his outfit wouldn't last long out there. 'Course they were drunk, and that might have been just talk. But you pass the word along, just keep my name out of it, Jim. I'd go bust if Evan Wells learned I sent Walt any such word and stopped trading with me."

"I'll have to tell Walt the source, if he asks," Jim replied.

"Him, but nobody else, you hear?"

"Nobody else," Jim Chaney said. Touching his heels to his mount, he headed for the Golden Bucket. The street was empty except for a few horses standing hipshot before the Golden Bucket and Riley's across the street.

Jim pulled up before the Golden Bucket, noting the W–in–a–Box brand on the other two horses already tied up there. He hesitated a moment, thinking perhaps he should cross the street to Riley's but then remembering Salty Sally, who worked at the Golden Bucket. He'd promised to come see her the next time he was in town. "Anyways," he said, shaking his head at the W–in–a–Box branded horses, "whoever's riding'em, I ain't scared of."

Swinging down, he wrapped his mount's reins about the hitch rail, swung a leg over, stepped up on the board-walk, and pushed through the butterfly doors. Two men, their back to the entrance, stood at an otherwise empty bar. The only other customers sat around a poker table where a game was in progress. From all appearances, the game had been an all night affair, because the players looked bleary–eyed and a little drunk.

Jim recognized two local ranchers and Jonas Pascal, a

professional gambler to whom Jim had lost a couple of paychecks. Jonas Pascal was a smart dresser and darkly handsome. He was rumored to be quite a lady's man, and Jim could see why women might find him attractive. The other player was a stranger, maybe a man from one of the mines up in the mountains; at least, he had that look about him.

"I'm all played out," one of the ranchers said and pushed back from the table as Jim passed.

"You interested in a game?" Pascal called to Jim.

"Ain't got the time," Jim said over his shoulder. "I just stopped in for a quick drink before I get back to the ranch."

"Too bad," Pascal said. "I could use some of that money Walt Davis' been passing around so freely."

At that comment, the two men at the bar turned and watched Jim approach the bar.

"Maybe another time," Jim replied, stopping before the bar. He rested a boot on the polished brass foot rail and his elbows on the freshly wiped bar.

"What'll it be?" asked Jake Bonner, the barkeep.

"A beer," Jim said and tossed a coin on the bar, "and is Sally working today?"

"Got the day off," Bonner said, reaching for a clean glass.

"Give 'im a sarsaparilla, Jake," one of the men to Jim's left said.

His companion snickered. "Or maybe a glass of buttermilk."

The remarks insulted his manhood, and Jim found it hard to ignore them, but he had promised Walt to stay out of trouble.

"You boys mind your own business," Jake Bonner said as he placed a glass of beer in front of the young man. "Jim's come in for a friendly drink and that's all."

Very few men, drunk or sober, messed with Jake Bonner. Weighing well above two hundred, Bonner was deep chested and stocky. His head was as smooth as a bowl, his eyes dark and penetrating under dark, bushy brows. His fleshy jowls and chin were always cleanly shaved, and he sported a black, well waxed mustache whose points curled upward to frame his bulbous nose.

"I ain't got no time for trouble, boys," Jim said. "I'm already due back at the ranch." He threw down his drink and headed for the swinging doors.

"I reckon your trouble's just starting," the older of the two men said. He was around thirty–five and wore a tied down gun in a cutback holster. He had deep-set eyes beneath barely visible brows. His eyes had the look of a rattler about to strike.

The remark, as intended, brought Jim up short. Turning back, he looked the speaker in the eye. "I ain't afraid of nothing or nobody," he said, "especially a gun hawk brought in by the likes of Evan Wells."

From behind the bar came the sound of a gun being cocked. "If you boys want to kill each other, take it out-side," Jake Bonner drawled.

Bonner held a sawed-off, double-barreled shotgun that waved menacingly back and forth between Jim and the W–in–a–Box men. "Hawley, that man rides for Walt Davis. You shoot him, and Walt Davis will come for you. If you want my advice, you better drop this right here. That goes for you too, Billings," Bonner said to the youngster with Hawley.

"Don't need any advice from you, Bonner," Ace Hawley snarled. "That's an uppity kid, and I intend to take him down a notch."

"Get outta here, Jim," Bonner said. "Ace, if you take a step after him, I'll blow your head off. Now go, Jim, or I might let *you* have one of these barrels!"

Jim, who could feel his heart pounding and a cold sweat beginning beneath his arms, knew he'd just been saved from a shootout that would have left him face down in the sawdust. Relieved that Jake Bonner had given him a face saving way out, Jim turned for the exit, forcing himself not to walk too fast.

Climbing aboard the dun, Jim rode north along the street. When he came to the crossing where he should turn west toward the mountains, he glanced back. Ace Hawley and his companion had just emerged from the Golden Bucket. They stared at him for a moment, mounted up, and rode south. *Reckon they ain't headed for home,* Jim thought to himself; the W–in–a–Box lay to the west in Jim's direction.

Jim kept a sharp lookout for the first few miles, afraid Ace Hawley and his companion might be lying in wait for him somewhere. When nothing happened, he relaxed, enjoying the sun on his back. A ground squirrel, tail curled in a loop over his back, raced across the trail. A few yards further on, a couple of red throated nuthatches flew up from a plot of brown grass at Jim's approach.

Jim was halfway home when a rifle exploded from the ridge to his right. The bullet hit the bay in the side and plowed through the horse's belly, mortally wounding the animal and sending it sideways to the ground. Jim threw himself from the saddle just in time to keep from being pinned down and scrambled wildly for the cover of a narrow ravine. He had gone only a few steps when something slammed into his back a few inches below his neck with such force that he was knocked forward five feet. He was dead before he hit the ground.

Walt worked till noon before he began to worry. "I think I better ride in and check on him," he said to Kell who worked nearby.

"He's a youngster, Walt," Kell replied. "Maybe he didn't stop at one drink. Maybe he got hooked up with one of Bonner's girls. He'll be home before long."

"I don't know, Kell," Walt replied. "Jim usually sticks to what he says he'll do, and he'd promised to be back before this. I think I'll ride in and check on him."

"Then I'll ride with you."

"Saddle us a mount while I step inside and tell Connie we might be late, or she'll wear that dinner bell out."

Kell had saddled his own mount and was tightening the cinch on Cougar when Walt returned. "What did she say?" he asked, knowing how much Connie Boyd hated keeping food warm when someone was late to eat one of her carefully prepared meals.

"She just gritted her teeth," Walt said and smiled.

"I stopped by and told Phil we'd be gone for awhile," Kell said. "He said he'd keep an eye out for trouble."

They were halfway to town when Walt spotted the circling buzzards. A chill like a cold breath of wind scampered along his spine. He pointed the vultures out to Kell.

"I saw them already," Kell said.

A half mile further on Walt spotted the bay. "That's his horse," he said and pointed toward the dead animal lying fifty feet off the trail. As they turned and approached the carcass, a couple of vultures flew up and flapped away. Stepping down, Walt stood over the horse, wondering what could have happened to Jim. Then he opened a bulging saddlebag and withdrew the sack of nails Jim had ridden to town for.

"He got to town and back to here," he said to Kell.

"There," Kell said, spotting Jim's body a few yards distant on the lip of a wash.

"He was trying to reach cover," Walt said.

They approached the body together, and kneeling, Walt saw the wound. "Back shot," he said softly. His face flushed angrily while, at the same time, he felt a sense of deep loss. Jim Chaney was too young to die like this. The youngster had become his friend, and, no doubt, he'd only been murdered because he worked for Walt. Still, he needed to make sure this was the work of the W–in–a–Box crew.

Rising, he looked around. "Must have come from that knoll over there," he said to Kell. "Reckon you could take him home across your mount?"

"No problem, but what're you gonna do?"

"Look around. See if I can find some tracks. If I find them, I'll see if they lead back to the W–in–a–Box."

"You ain't gonna do anything foolish?" asked Kell. "I had come to like the kid too. I want in on any action."

"I'll just try to find out where they went," Walt replied.

Walt helped Kell get Jim's body aboard Kell's mount and watched as his foreman rode off in the direction of home. Then, climbing aboard Cougar, he sent the stallion toward the knoll. He found plenty of signs on the crest of the hillock. Impressions of where two men had lain were clearly visible, and two empty cartridge shells had been left behind. Further down the slope and out of sight of the trail, fairly fresh horse apples told him they'd left their horses tied up to a scrubby oak.

Walt took a moment to study the few prints left behind after someone's ineffective attempt to erase them by sweeping a brush about. One was narrow and long, the other more average in shape, and both had been freshly shoed. Walt would remember the narrow print if he ever saw it again. The trail of the dragged brush headed straight for the W–in–a–Box, but he followed a ways to make sure.

"Bastards," Walt muttered.

He badly wanted to ride after them, but he restrained

his fury. Whatever he did must be carefully planned, or he'd suffer Jim's fate. At the moment, that didn't seem so bad as long as he took Evan Wells and the men who had shot Jim Chaney with him. Turning Cougar about, he rode after Kell.

Chapter Fourteen

Walt, Kell Franklin, and Phil Boyd pushed back from an early supper, thanked Connie for a fine meal, and wandered out to the front porch of the now finished cabin when darkness began to fall. Kell lowered himself to the front steps and rolled a cigarette. Phil Boyd leaned in the open doorway and rolled a smoke of his own. Walt walked to the edge of the front porch and stared at the dark, purplish outline of the Rockies.

"You've been awfully quiet since we buried Jim," Kell Franklin called in Walt's direction after he had lit his smoke.

"I think I'll ride into town," Walt replied. "I'd like to find out if Jim had a run in with some of Wells' men while he was there. Maybe I can get a line on who ambushed him."

"Want me to ride in with you?" asked Kell.

"Or me?" asked Phil Boyd.

"No, I'd like the two of you to stay here and look after things."

"Why? You planning to stay in town awhile?" asked Kell.

"I don't know how long I'll be," Walt said. "Depends on what I find, but the two of you should be on the alert. Wells might decide to hit us anytime."

"We'll keep our eyes open," Kell said. "You be careful too."

Walt didn't reply. Turning, he passed by Phil Boyd, who remained in the doorway, and found his hat and set it squarely on his head. His six-gun hung from the back of a straight chair set against the wall. He strapped the gun on and took the Winchester from the rack over the fireplace. Leaving the cabin, he passed by Phil and Kell without speaking.

Cougar caught his smell and came to the corral fence as Walt approached. The animal reminded Walt of the grulla he had left behind in the canyon, and he recalled the peace he had enjoyed there. Maybe someday, he could return there, he thought to himself.

Catching up Cougar, he led him from the corral and laid on his gear. As he rode from the yard in the direction of Prentiss, he saw that Phil had moved out to sit on the steps beside Kell.

Two of the best, Walt thought to himself, as he rode past the cabin. Mustn't let the same thing that happened to Jim happen to either of them.

As he passed beneath the cottonwood, he noticed the mound of fresh dirt that was Jim's grave. He pulled up and stared down at the grave for a moment. Jim Chaney had been young, fresh, and exuberant and, somehow, Walt felt responsible for his death. Earlier that day he had carried out the most difficult chore of his life. He had written Jim's mother in Kansas and told her of her only son's death.

Darkness settled in as Walt rode toward Prentiss. Overhead, the sky blazed with stars, and a pale sickle moon made a curved slash on the horizon. An occasional nighthawk, searching for mosquitoes, zoomed overhead, the swoosh of his wings loud in the silent, starry night.

Except for the lights from the two saloons, Prentiss' main street was dark as he rode in. Horses crowded the hitchracks before each establishment, and the sounds of drunken laughter flowed freely from both. Walt decided to try Riley's first. Entering, he looked around, seeing a few familiar faces, but none he recognized as belonging to the W–in–a–Box. Pushing through to the bar, he waited for John Freshly, the owner and bartender, to approach.

"What's your poison, Walt?" he asked.

"A little information," replied Walt.

"If I can," Freshly said.

"Was my rider, Jim Chaney, in today, John?"

"Today? No, and I was in early and haven't left since. Why? That youngster run out on you?"

"No, I sent him into town this morning, and he was ambushed and killed on his way back."

"Tarnation, Walt! Who would do a thing like that? I wouldn't have thought Jim Chaney had an enemy in the world."

"I don't think he did, John," Walt replied. "I think who-ever shot him was my enemy."

Caution immediately crept into John Freshly's face. "Sorry I can't be of more help," he said and looked about carefully. When a customer down the bar called for anoth-er drink, John Freshly seemed relieved and moved quick-ly to wait on him.

Evan Wells has got everyone buffaloed, Walt thought to himself. After a moment, he left Riley's and crossed the street to the Golden Bucket. As he pushed through the swinging doors, he could barely see through the smoky haze, and the smell of sour beer drifted up from the sawdust floor. Walt stood just inside and looked the place over.

Andy Chandler, the piano player, came through a door to the side of the bar. When he sat down at the piano, his nimble fingers did a tinkling run over the keys.

"Gentlemen!" he called. "The Golden Bucket has a treat for you tonight. Let me introduce you to our new singer, Maudie Barry. Let's give her a welcoming round of applause!" Andy Chandler led the handclapping as Maudie Barry swept through the same side door.

The change was startling, and Walt hardly recognized her. Her hair was swept back and up, held in place by a couple of sparkling combs. She wore a low-cut, green silk gown that glistened even in the dim, smoky light and exposed every seductive curve of her body. Greenish ear bobs and a beaded necklace matched the dress. Somebody, Walt decided, had spent a small bundle on that dress, and he wondered if some of his own money had gone toward paying for it.

Jonas Pascal, the handsome gambler, sat at the nearest table and applauded enthusiastically. Before Maudie began to sing, the two exchanged a look. Obviously, they had developed a quick friendship, or something even more intimate, Walt decided.

"Now the Golden Bucket's newest song bird will give us her rendition of 'Only A Bird In Gilded Cage,' " Andy announced. And Maudie, with a surprisingly soft but strong voice, began to sing.

Walt heard several clearing of throats and a few audible sighs as Maudie sang the sad lyrics. When the last note was sounded, the men burst into whistles and applause, shouting for more, but Maudie turned from the piano and exited through the same door from which she had entered.

"She'll be back for more later, folks," Andy Chandler shouted and then began to pound out "Camp Town Races" on the piano.

Jake Bonner met him as Walt approached the bar. "What'll you have, Walt?" he asked.

"Did a hand of mine drop in today for a drink, Jake?" Walt asked.

"Jim Chaney. This morning. Soon after I opened up." Bonner replied.

"Was there some kind of trouble, Jake?"

"Yeah, he had words with two of Wells' men, Ace Hawley and Josh Billings."

"What happened?"

"I think Wells' men would have killed him if I hadn't stepped in," replied Bonner. "They were ready to box him when I took Old Bessie out and held them off. I told Jim to ride. I let Hawley and Billings go a few minutes after your man left."

"That's all you know?" asked Walt.

"That's all. Did something happen to Chaney?" the barkeep asked.

"He was ambushed and killed about halfway back to the ranch," Walt replied.

"Sorry to hear that," Bonner said, and Walt saw something of the same caution in Bonner's face as he'd seen in John Freshly's. "But you might try asking Billings," Bonner continued. "That's him talking to my new singer, Maudie, at the end of the bar."

Josh Billings felt their eyes on him and looked in their direction, his gaze fastening on Walt. Billings' nicely formed features belied the knavery beneath, but he had almost colorless eyes and, at the moment, a tight, drawn look. As the two men faced each other, the saloon, including the piano, went silent. Stepping back from the bar, Josh Billings turned to face Walt.

"I got a question for you, Billings," Walt said, his voice carrying to every corner of the saloon.

"Ain't my day to be questioned," Billings replied, "but you can ask anyway."

"Did you and Ace Hawley waylay and shoot Jim Chaney?" Walt asked.

"I don't know nothing about no ambush," Billings replied.

"I think you do," Walt said. "You and Hawley had a run–in with him in here this morning. You were seen following him when he left town."

"Those are lies."

"You tried to brush out the prints of your horses," Walt continued, "but I found a few. One print was long and narrow. I guess you wouldn't mind if we went out and took a look at your horse's hoofs?"

Walt had hardly finished speaking before Josh Billings went for his gun. Billings got off the first shot, but he had rushed it. Walt felt the hot air of the bullet zip past his ear. He squeezed off a shot then, not aiming to kill but to wound, and Billings was knocked back as Walt's bullet struck him in the shoulder of his gun arm. Billings gave a loud grunt of pain and flopped up and down a couple of times.

Walt, gun in hand, crossed to where Billings lay and looked down at him. Cocking the Peacemaker again, he placed the barrel against Billings' forehead. "You want to live?" he asked.

"It was Hawley's idea!" Billings whined, his face white with pain from the shoulder wound. "I swear to God! Hawley did the shooting!"

"You're a sniveling coward, Billings!" Walt said as he yanked Billings to his feet. "Is your horse outside?"

"Yeah," Billings managed.

"You get on him, and ride down to Doc's and get yourself fixed up. Then you better ride fast and far. If I ever see you again, I'll kill you. You understand me?"

"I understand," Billings said, his voice barely above a whisper.

Billings' six–gun lay at his feet. Walt picked it up, emptied the remaining cartridge on the sawdust floor, and rammed the gun into Billings' holster. "Don't reload it till you're well out of town," he said.

Those who had witnessed the episode watched as Billings shambled from the saloon. They were silent and ashamed for the once boastful young gunslinger. They knew his life would never be the same, that the episode they'd just witnessed would follow Billings wherever he went in the West.

"Drinks on the house!" Jake Bonner announced, breaking the silence.

Walt pushed through the crowd that swarmed toward the bar and walked outside. Josh Billings, bent over his horse's neck and outlined in the dim moonlight, was a half a block down the street and heading for the doctor's house a block further on. Walt stepped over the hitchrack and stood beside Cougar a moment. He watched Billings turn in at the doctor's house. Then he swung onto Cougar's saddle and headed for home.

Chapter Fifteen

"You're late for breakfast again, as usual!" Ezra Dudley growled as Misty came down the stairs a full two hours after the ranchhands had eaten.

"Sorry, Ezra," Misty said, kissing the old cook on the cheek. "Anyway, I'll just have coffee. When I'm finished, I want you to do me a favor."

"What favor?"

"I'm moving into town today, Ezra," Misty replied. "I've already packed. I just need someone to drive me into town. Would you do me that favor?"

"I reckon," the old man said.

"Then hitch a horse to a buggy and bring it up to the front of the house."

"I didn't think your uncle would allow it," Ezra said.

"He has no choice in the matter," Misty replied. "I'm of age, and I have money of my own. If you're afraid of making Uncle Evan mad with you, I'll understand. After all, he's the one who pays you."

Ezra gave an even louder snort. "I ain't afraid of the devil himself!" he declared. "I'll have a buggy at the front door in ten minutes."

"And Checkers belongs to me," Misty told him. "Saddle him and bring him along. I'll go up and get my bag and meet you out front."

A few minutes later, Misty came down the stairs carrying a stuffed portmanteau containing all the clothes she had brought with her from the East and a few items she had bought since in Prentiss. She had decided that rather than risk a scene with her uncle, she would leave without telling him. The note she had written would explain everything. Once in the hallway, she dropped the note on a reception table and continued on.

As she passed the study door, she was stopped momentarily by her uncle's angry voice. "I won't let him get away with running one of my men out of the state," Evan Wells was saying. "If I do, soon every small rancher and farmer in the territory will think they can stand up to me! No, I want Walt Davis dead. You understand me, Ace?"

"Yes, sir. How many men should I take on the raid?"

"As many as you think you need, but I wouldn't think you'd need more than ten or twelve. There's only three of them and a woman."

"They're all good fighters, Mr. Wells," Ace Hawley replied, "and they'll be forted up. Won't be like we were meeting them face to face."

"They won't be behind barricades if you take them by surprise," Evan Wells said. "And don't come back here and tell me you didn't shoot him. If you can't kill 'im, I'll find someone who can, and you won't draw any more fat paychecks from me."

Though there was a door between them, Misty could picture her uncle's stern, cruel face as he gave the orders; his gray–green eyes would be fiery, his face dark with anger. As Misty crept from the house, she had only one thought in mind. She couldn't stand by and let her uncle murder innocent people. She had to warn Walt Davis.

"What's happened to you, honey?" Ezra asked when Misty came from the house.

She put the portmanteau in the buggy. "I don't have time to tell you," she said. "Take my bag into Prentiss. Leave it at the hotel." She swung into the saddle and, slapping Checkers' neck, sent him in a gallop out of the yard.

"Now what's got into her?" old Ezra asked and, puzzled, watched until Misty was out of sight. Stepping into the buggy, he was pulling out of the yard when Ace Hawley came from the house.

"Where're you going, old man?" Hawley yelled.

"None of you daggoned business!" yelled Ezra and slapped the horse with the reins, putting him into a trot.

"You better get back here, old man!" Hawley shouted. "Cook up a good meal. Me and the boys will be awful hungry when we get back from this job."

If Ezra heard him, he paid no attention. He was wondering if the job Hawley was talking about had anything to do with Misty's sudden distress.

Knowing Ace Hawley and her uncle's men would be close behind, Misty pushed Checkers hard. She hoped Walt and his men would be near the house when she got there. Even so, they'd have little time to prepare.

The mid-morning sun was hot on her neck as she urged Checkers on. In the distance, a wind devil traced an erratic path across the range, lifting dust and debris into a whirling circle. Off to her right, a half dozen antelopes threw up their heads and, frightened by the onrushing horse and rider, scrambled away.

Misty drew up well away from the buildings and waited for whoever was there to recognize her. Giving a sigh of relief when she saw three men come from the corral, and recognizing Walt among them, she urged Checkers on one more time.

"What's wrong, Misty?" Walt asked, grabbing the reins of the foam flecked pony. "The devil chasing you?"

"Maybe worse," Misty replied as Walt helped her down. "You haven't got much time. Ace Hawley and a dozen of my uncle's men are on their way here now. They have orders to kill you."

Walt had been expecting such an attack for a long time. "Thanks for the warning," he said to Misty. "Now you better ride out before they come."

"Checkers wouldn't make it another half mile," she said.

"Then take Cougar," Walt urged.

"No, I think I'll stick around," Misty told him.

Walt looked frustrated for a moment. "Kell," he said, turning to his foreman, "saddle four horses. Take them and Misty's mount up to the spring. Be sure you have your rifle and plenty of ammunition. Take along as many supplies as you can grab in a hurry. And keep Evan's men off the slope. If they attack from that advantage, we won't stand a chance. Have the horses ready if we have to make a run for it."

"You got it, Boss," Kell replied and went into action.

"You and me will hold them off from the front," he told Phil Boyd. "Pick yourself a barricade, and I'll take another." Turning to Misty, he said, "Connie's in the house. Tell her what's about to happen, and the two of you stay inside."

Misty, who had taken her rifle from its scabbard before Kell led Checkers away, nodded and ran for the cabin. She had barely reached the front door when, looking back, she saw riders pull up a couple of hundred yards out.

"What's happening?" Connie asked, opening the door behind Misty.

"My uncle's sent his men to kill Walt," Misty

explained. "I rode here to warn him. That's Uncle Evan's men up there now."

"Bless you, child," Connie Boyd said and pulled Misty inside. Grabbing a rifle from a rack on the wall, she said, "I don't suppose you'll want to fight your uncle's men, but Phil's out there. I don't intend to stand by and let them kill my man."

"I don't look upon him as kin anymore," Misty replied. "I'll take this window. You take the other."

Walt saw Ace Hawley give the order for his men to dismount and continue on foot. "And keep low," Hawley shouted, leading the way.

The gang came in shifts. One shift kept up a withering fire which hampered any return fire, while the other, running low, and using whatever cover was available, pressed forward. Then the maneuver was repeated all over again.

"We don't stand a chance, Phil!" Walt yelled. "We best make a run for it! We'll collect the women and try and make it up the slope to where Kell is. If they try to follow, Kell can pick them off."

"But where will we go?" Phil Boyd asked as he scrambled from the hole and ran for the cabin.

"To the mountains!" Walt replied from a few feet behind.

A furious fusillade of bullets kicked up dirt all around them as they ran, stopping only when they reached the cover of the cabin. Then the log walls took the brunt of the attack. Hoping Kell had all the supplies they'd need for several days, Walt yelled for everyone to follow, and they exited the cabin's back door and continued their run up the slope to where Kell fired shot after shot at any W-in-a-Box man who tried to follow.

Ace Hawley and his men took shelter in front of the cabin and the outbuildings. As Walt watched, tendrils of smoke trailed up from both buildings. *That's twice Evan Wells has burned me out*, he thought to himself.

"You're hit!" Connie Boyd cried, noticing the blood dripping from Phil's leg. Scrambling down, she ran to her husband to examine the wound.

"A flesh wound," Phil said.

"You need a tourniquet to help stop the bleeding," Connie told him. Taking no notice of the men, she flipped her skirt up and tore off a long strip of her petticoat and wound it tightly around Phil's leg several times. "That'll help," she said, "but if it gets any worse, we'll have to stop and seal up the wound."

"You sure you can ride, Phil?" Walt asked. "If you can't, we'll make our stand here."

"You lead the way, Boss," replied Boyd, "and I won't be far behind."

"You sure you want to go with us?" Walt asked, turning to Misty. "You can ride out now and tell your uncle we forced you to take a hand in this. But if you go with us, you won't be able to return."

"Why?" asked Misty.

"You wouldn't do it intentionally, but Evan Wells is a determined man. He might force you to lead him to us."

"I would never do such a thing!"

"A person never knows what they'll do when pressured enough, but make up your mind now."

"I'm coming with you," Misty replied.

"Kell, you hang back and discourage any pursuit," Walt instructed his foreman. "The rest of you follow me."

"Where're we going?" asked Phil Boyd.

"To a place I know in the mountains," Walt replied.

Chapter Sixteen

They rode till near sundown, stopping only to give the horses a breather every hour or so. Finally, Walt pulled up at a limestone sink surrounded by cottonwoods. "The water may be a little bitter," he said, "but we'll camp here tonight. Connie, reckon you and Misty could cook us up some food while I see to Phil's leg."

"You leave the cooking to us and look after my Phil," Connie replied.

"Put your arm around my shoulders," he told Phil when he'd helped him dismount and, half carrying him, sat Phil down on a log. "You'll either have to pull your pants down, or I'll have to cut the pants leg off," he said.

"Happens these are all I brought with me," Phil replied. He unbuckled his belt and slipped his pants down

"Don't reckon you brought along any more underwear, either?" Walt asked.

"You tell the ladies not to look, and I'll pull them down too."

"Don't be ridiculous, Phillip Boyd!" Connie scolded from nearby. "Who wants to see your hairy body anyway?"

"The wound doesn't look too bad," Walt said after he had examined Phil's leg. "And I can stop the bleeding."

He went to a nearby patch of prickly pears and cut off a big leaf and, roasting the leaf over the fire to burn off the spines, tied it over the wound with piggin strings.

"Where did you learn that?" asked Kell, who had just ridden in.

"From an Indian medicine man," Walt replied. "He said he used it to fight inflammation. I figure it'll also help to clot the bleeding."

Meanwhile, Connie had emptied a couple of cans of beef into a skillet. Leaving Misty to stir the meat, Connie gathered wild onions, some breadroot, and a few bulbs of sego lily from around the camp area and dropped them in with the beef to give the meal some bulk. Soon the aroma of cooking stew permeated the campsite.

Finishing the meal, they sat around the campfire and talked. "What's this place you're taking us to?" asked Phil who was feeling much better after a hot meal.

"I stumbled across it after I killed Ford Wells and was chased into the mountains by the W–in–a–Box crew," replied Walt. "You'll have to see it to believe it, so I won't try to tell you about it. If we can cover our tracks as we ride in, we should be free of Wells' outfit as long as we stay there."

"How high in the mountains?" asked Kell.

"Almost to the top of the Divide," replied Walt.

"What about game?" asked Phil. "We'll need food."

"Most any kind you can ask for," Walt told him.

"I would never call you a liar, Walt," Kell said, "but I never heard of animals that high up. You sure you haven't dreamed this place instead of actually being there?"

"You'll see," was all Walt would say.

They finished the stew, and Connie and Misty gathered up the dishes, scrubbing them with sand and rinsing them off in the stream. From high in the mountains the faint wail of a wolf drifted down, and Walt thought of the wolf in the canyon and wondered if the old loner had got wanderlust and left his home turf.

"Gives me the shivers," Connie said as she and Misty returned to the fire.

"I think we better post a guard," Walt said, glancing at his companions. "We don't want anyone slipping up on us while we sleep." He glanced at Phil. "Looks like it's up to me and you," he said to Kell.

"No, I'll take my turn," Phil insisted. "I wouldn't be able to sleep much anyway with this leg. It'll do just as well with me sitting out there on a rock somewhere."

"Nonsense," Walt scolded. "You mustn't do any walking. You'll start the wound bleeding all over again."

Phil wanted to protest, but he acquiesced, saying, "I reckon you're right."

They doused the fire and had spread their bedrolls before the sun was fully set. As Walt strolled out to take the first watch, the others crawled into their bedrolls. "Call me at midnight," Kell called to Walt.

Walt scrambled up a head-high boulder and sat, facing east. As the rolling plains stretching toward Denver were closed down with darkness, he saw the flickering light of a campfire in the distance. If that was the Wells outfit, and he felt sure it was, they couldn't be more than three miles out. He considered riding out and putting a few bullets into the camp, but decided the time was still not right for a counter strike. *Maybe in the mountains, if they can't be shaken*, he decided.

Walt's thoughts turned to Misty Wells. He was surprised at the way she had made herself at home in the group. She had constantly given Connie a hand at cooking and cleaning, which was surprising for a woman who was probably used to being waited on. Nor had she been a drag on the trail, keeping up easily and hiding the weariness she must have suffered. Why had she insisted on coming along? She and her uncle must have had quite a run–in. But how long would she be satisfied to hide out in the mountains without the luxuries she was used to on her uncle's ranch? And what would he do if, once settled in the canyon, she decided she wanted to head back to Prentiss? Would he let her go? Could he afford to?

The fire out on the prairie had long since gone out when Kell came out a little after midnight to relieve Walt.

"They're out there," Walt informed Kell and told him about the fire. "Get us up well before daylight, and we'll leave without cooking. If we can see their fire, they could see ours. Anyway, I expect there'll be some leftovers we can chew on as we ride. We'll put as much distance as possible between us and them before they wake up and get moving."

The travel up the mountains was arduous but uneventful. Walt led the way, keeping to solid rock whenever possible. Still, he knew that, whatever the surface, horseshoe prints could be easily followed.

Kell continued to bring up the rear, destroying any tracks left behind whenever possible. There had been no further sign of pursuit since they'd spotted the gang's campfire and Walt was hoping the Wells riders had given up and turned back, but he knew he couldn't depend on that.

When they reached the canyon, Walt pulled up and let the others gather round him. "There it is," he said, indicating the deep, seemingly impregnable canyon.

His companions gazed silently into the canyon's depth for a moment. The deer grazed peacefully beside the small trickle of water coming from the spring. The weariness in Walt seemed to slip away as he gazed down upon the familiar scene.

"I never seen anything like it. It's all you said and more, Walt," Kell said.

"It's beautiful," Misty added.

"How're we gonna get down there?" asked the ever practical Connie.

"There's a ledge," replied Walt, "but too narrow to ride down. We'll have to go down on foot and lead the horses." He turned to Phil Boyd. "Reckon your leg will be up to it?"

"Practically healed," replied Phil. "Just lead the way."

Walt knew better than to believe that Phil had recovered from the wound so quickly, but he let it slide. "Then follow me," he said, and led the way around the canyon to the ledge.

Before starting down, he helped Phil Boyd astride Cougar. "Get a good grip on the horn," he told Phil. "Make sure you don't get the inside leg squeezed against the cliff. Reckon it's a good thing the hurt leg will be on the outside going down." Then, slowly and carefully, he began the descent, the others following just as carefully behind him.

Once at the bottom, the group was welcomed by whinnies from the grulla and the mare, who trotted in to rub noses with Cougar and to receive friendly rubs from Walt, who had worried about leaving them in territory claimed by the big grizzly. But both animals were fat and sleek and looked in top condition.

Everyone, including Walt, took a moment to let their eyes wander up the steep cliffs. "Feels a touch like a prison," Connie muttered to Misty.

"What keeps us in will keep others out," Misty reminded her.

"We gonna build some shelter?" Kell asked Walt.

"No, for the time being, we're gonna leave everything looking as natural as we can. Later on we may build, depending on how long we have to stay here. But we won't sleep in the open. There are several caves at the foot of the cliffs, one of which was my home while I was here. We'll install Connie and Phil in there and look around for a place for the rest of us. The main thing," he continued, "is that when someone looks into the canyon, they see nothing that suggests there is anyone living here. Whatever you do, keep that in mind.

"The first thing to do is turn the horses loose to graze," Walt continued, "but I should warn you. The biggest grizzly I ever saw claims this valley too. Always keep an eye out; he's a monster, and he won't be easy to kill. And there's a loner wolf too. He won't bother us, so don't shoot him. It was his home long before it became ours."

"What about Misty?" asked Connie.

"What about her?" Walt asked.

"You don't expect her to sleep out till you find a place for her and fix it up," Connie scolded. "She'll live with Phil and me till then. That all right with you, honey?"

"Perfectly," replied Misty.

Walt and Kell settled into a cave nearby and, as the days passed, the group settled into a routine. Phil's wound healed rapidly in the clean mountain air, and he was soon able to join in the work required to keep Connie and Misty supplied with firewood as well as pile up a supply if winter came and found them still in the canyon. The work of cutting wood went slow, since they had to leave no sign when they felled a tree. The same with the trees already down.

Keeping that in mind, each tree felled for wood was cut off evenly with the ground and dirt sprinkled over the fresh stump to hide it. Unused branches and limbs were burned at night when the smoke wouldn't show and the ashes carefully scattered when they cooled.

Walt chose to do the hunting for meat, killing only

when meat supplies ran low. He carefully saved the hides, cleaned them, and stretched them out to dry. They'd need them for clothes if they had to stay in the canyon very long. Hides could also be used in other ways, for water bags, to hold nuts and seeds when gathered, and there were numerous other needs about a camp.

There was no dearth of volunteers to fish for trout in the lake, and the fish provided a welcome change from venison, rabbit, and squirrel. To save ammunition, these were caught in the same traps Walt had used during his earlier stay.

Phil, a handy builder, began working on furniture to make the caves more comfortable. Selecting young oak saplings, he stripped them of bark and let them cure. Then he cut them into lengths to fit the vision in his head. He fit them together by interlocking notches he had cut into the wood and then made glue from the horns of a buck and used it to reinforce the notches. The seat was made from cured deer skin. The first finished product looked cumbersome, but Connie, showing confidence in her husband, proudly lowered her weight into the chair.

"Beats sitting on a rock by miles," she said, and smiled at Phil. "You must build us a bed next," she announced proudly.

"After a few more chairs," Phil said and gave her a knowing smile.

Chapter Seventeen

Ace Hawley, a man who had made his living with his gun, had fought in range wars from Texas to Montana and points in between. He prided himself on being the equal of any man, and there were few he had feared. Yet he had always been edgy in the presence of Evan Wells.

He had put off reporting back to the ranch for several days while his men combed the foothills and the slopes of the Rockies. Walt Davis and his party had simply vanished. Knowing Evan Wells would grow more and more impatient for word of the outcome, Hawley finally called off the search and led the men back to the W–in–a–Box.

Evan Wells' reaction was a stony silence. Rising from the desk in his study, he paced back and forth a couple of times. "And my niece?" he asked. "Did you find her?"

"She was with them," replied Hawley. "Even did some shooting when we attacked the ranch."

"The little traitor!" Wells swore. "She's no longer my kin. She'll pay just like the others when we find them. And we've got to find them! Walt Davis will be a thorn in my flesh until he's dead. Word will already be spreading that he defied me and got away with it. Others will drum up the nerve to do the same. Walt Davis and everyone with him have to be eliminated."

"Yes, sir," Hawley agreed meekly.

"You ever hear of a man named Buster Alison?" asked Wells.

"I've heard of him," Hawley replied. "Saw him slice a man to ribbons with a Bowie knife up in Kansas. But Alison's an old man now, ain't he?"

"He may be old, but he's still tough as nails," Wells said. "I stopped off for a night in Spenser Creek, Kansas on my last trip to St. Louis. Saw him in a saloon. He's the man for this job."

"Why do you think an old buffer skinner could find Davis when me and the men searched just about every nook and cranny this side of the Continental Divide?" Ace Hawley suddenly realized he might be replaced as top dog on the W–in–a–Box if Alison came aboard. He didn't like the idea, didn't like it at all, but there was nothing he could do about it at the moment.

"Buster Alison was born in those mountains," Wells said. "He roamed the Rockies with some of the old timers, like Hickok and Cody. Word was he could shoot with the best of them when he wasn't using that big knife. Alison knows every canyon and valley up there. He's the man to find Davis and take care of him."

Wells went to the wall safe and, keeping himself between the safe and Hawley, twisted the knob back and forth a few times and pulled the door open. Taking out a bundle of hundred dollar bills, he counted out twenty-one. He placed the bundle once again in the safe, spun the knob, and turned back to Hawley. "But he don't come cheap," he said and, turning to Hawley, counted out two thousand dollars. "Find Alison, give him the money. Tell him there's another two thousand when he brings me proof of Davis' death."

"Four thousand dollars!" Hawley said. "My God . . . !"

"And here is a hundred for your expenses," Wells added, giving Hawley another bill. "Now get out of here, and I don't want to see your face till you can tell me Buster Alison is on the job."

"Yes, sir," Hawley said and, reaching for his hat, pocketed the money and left the room.

After a few discreet inquiries among various acquaintances, Hawley got the word that Alison still hung out in Spenser Creek when he needed a rest from his itinerant wanderings. Hawley took the next stage east.

The stage was two days out of Denver with only Hawley and a drummer for passengers when a man on foot signaled the stage to stop. "Been waiting for you all day," he said to Rowdy Stover, the aging driver. "Need a ticket to St. Louis."

"I ain't got time to sell you a ticket now," Rowdy told him. "Get aboard, and I'll write you a ticket at the next stop."

The man's draw was sudden and swift. "Just step down, old timer, and that goes for the two of you in the stage," he added, waving his gun back and forth between the driver and the stage. The man was lean and wiry with hungry, demanding eyes. He wore a dusty black coat, and his now empty holster was tied low on his thigh.

Hawley suddenly realized the position he was in. He was carrying two thousand dollars of Wells' money and maybe three hundred of his own. Old man Wells would never believe he'd lost the money in a holdup. He'd swear Hawley had lost it gambling. Nor did Hawley have the nerve to return all the way to Prentiss and try to tell Wells the money had been lost. Wells just might decide he no longer had any use for a gunman who let himself be held up.

As Hawley stepped from the stage, he drew his own gun and shot the robber in the heart. The man staggered back a few steps, a surprised look on his face, and he slowly wilted to the ground, like a weed long without water.

"I ain't never seen better shooting, mister," Stover said, "nor more timely, either. Let me thank you."

"Time for that later," Hawley said. "Better get going. There might be more of them."

Rowdy Stover snapped his whip over the backs of the four span, and the horses responded. In seconds they were in a gallop, the stage careening down the trail with the wheels throwing up tails of dust. Old Stover kept them running for at least another mile before he pulled up to let them rest. Fortunately, nothing else happened along the way, and two days later, the stage pulled into Spenser Creek.

Hawley found Buster Alison in Spenser Creek's only saloon. Alison was a big man. His iron-gray hair poked haphazardly from beneath a seedy looking Davy Crockett coonskin cap and the accompanying ratty coon tail. He had moody dark eyes and a bony nose that appeared to have been broken, maybe more than once. A thick graying, tobacco–stained beard covered the lower part of his face.

Men at the bar stood apart from him, and Hawley knew why as he approached and caught a whiff of the man's greasy buckskin pants and pullover buckskin shirt. *My God, he stinks,* Hawley thought to himself. Must not have had a bath for years.

Hawley eyed the black-handled Bowie hanging prominently from Alison's belt, and a Mills .75 pistol converted to a four-shot revolver protruded from a worn leather holster on Alison's hip. All of seventeen inches long, the gun looked fit to break a man's wrist with the recoil.

Another weapon, a fourteen-pound Sharps .45 with a thick octagonal barrel, stood against the bar at Alison's side.

"You Buster Alison?" Hawley asked, stopping a couple of steps away and trying not to inhale the man's odor.

Buster Alison turned baleful eyes on the questioner. "Who wants to know?" he asked in in a gravelly, whiskey–soaked voice.

"Ace Hawley. You may have heard of me."

"Can't say I have."

"I've been sent with a proposition for you, a very rewarding proposition that could make you a rich man," Hawley said. He was disappointed his name meant nothing to Alison.

This got Alison's attention, and he softened his demeanor perceptively. "Just how rewarding?" he asked.

"Two thousand up front, and two more when the job is finished."

For a moment, Alison's dark eyes seemed to slice through Hawley as effectively as his famous knife. "Come with me," he growled and led the way to a vacant table. Pulling back a chair and sitting, he gave Hawley another glare. "Talk," he ordered.

"You ever hear of Evan Wells?" asked Hawley.

"The big Colorado rancher?"

"The same."

"Who does he want me to kill? Must be one tough hombre to offer me four thousand dollars."

"Maybe not so tough, but hard to find," Hawley said.

"Ain't no man I can't find if he's living," Alison said. "Tell me about this man who's worth four thousand dollars dead."

"His name is Walt Davis, and he's hid out in the mountains above Prentiss," Hawley replied.

"Right up my alley," Alison said. "I know them mountains like the back of my hand. Give me the up-front money."

Hawley counted out the cash, and Buster Alison licked his lips greedily as the stack of bills grew. Hawley doubted the man had ever possessed so much money at any one time in his life. For that matter, few men west of the Mississippi had.

"Now tell me what this Davis fella looks like," said Alison as he put the money away.

Hawley gave a detailed description, having studied Davis carefully over the weeks and months.

"You tell Wells I'll see him in a few days if not before," Alison said and bellowed for the barkeep to bring him a bottle.

"Mr. Wells wants you now," Hawley insisted. "Why don't you ride the stage back with me?"

"The point is not to be seen with you or anyone else that would connect me to Wells," replied Alison. "I'll just slip in, get rid of Davis, and slip out again. But I won't forget to pick up the rest of my money, and you tell Wells what will happen to him if he tries to welch on the rest after the job is done."

"You have to show him proof it was Davis you killed," Alison reminded him.

"You tell Wells I'll bring him Davis' head in a sack."

Buster Alison decided to take the train back to Denver. He needed his horses in Prentiss, and he didn't want to waste the time required to ride to Denver on horseback. Stepping down from the passenger car before the train had come to a full stop, he walked back to a cattle car and watched as a tender unloaded his horses, a small bay mare and an already saddled gelding—a big, dark gray, spare-ribbed animal who looked as capable of violence as his master. Swinging into the saddle, Alison rode along main street to the mercantile.

Once inside, he purchased a dozen cans of beef, as many cans of beans, and a sack of potatoes. His final purchase was a sack of grain for his horses. He paid the merchant with a hundred dollar bill and watched with amusement as the man emptied both his cash drawer and his pockets to make change. His next stop was Dempsters Saloon where he purchased three bottles of Kentucky whiskey. Hawley had given him directions to Prentiss, and Alison set out for that town at once, intending to bypass the town rather than ride through it. He also had some idea of where Davis and his bunch had entered the mountains. Alison, astride the big gray and leading his pack mare, sent the big horse in that direction.

Chapter Eighteen

Several days passed, and Misty Wells' comment about the carpetbaggers in Virginia stayed with Walt. What if Wells were pressed on all sides by families settling on land that Wells had not filed on? The families would need help until they brought a crop in or raised enough cattle to sell, but Walt not only had sixty thousand dollars in the Prentiss bank going unused, he knew where he could put his hand on plenty more if needed. In fact, he had been to the spot where he'd found the gold several times since returning to the canyon.

The first step, he decided, was to take Kell and Phil into his confidence. With that in mind, he asked them to take a walk with him about the canyon and, leading them to the spring, told them of the gold buried beneath the pile of boulders.

"Anything you take out will belong to all of us," Walt told them, "but I want to put some into fighting Evan Wells. He's flown too high for too long in Colorado. I want to clip his wings."

"What've you got in mind?" asked Kell.

"I want you and Phil to roll those boulders away and begin the digging again."

"What about you?" asked Phil.

Walt told them of the money in the Prentiss bank. "I intend to use that for loans to men who'll settle on any unclaimed land in and around the W-in-a-Box. Before I make a man a loan, he'll have to promise to join all the others in making a stand against Wells if and when Wells makes a move on anyone. If I need more money, I'd like to use some of the gold the two of you take out."

"That suits me," Kell said, "but that'll mean a range war. A lot of men are going to be killed."

"A lot of men have already been killed," replied Walt, "by hired guns brought in by Wells. Like Ace Hawley. How many settlers has he killed? Maybe we can rid Colorado of Hawley and all the others like him. What about you, Phil?"

"Count me in," Phil said, "but I hope there's some gold left for me and Connie to buy us a little place to settle down on. Connie wants kids, and we need a place that'll bring in enough to keep them fed."

"There'll be enough," Walt said. "We'll see to it."

"That's all a fella can ask," replied Phil.

"When you uncover the gold, make sure you scatter the dirt so as to leave the place looking natural. Remember Evan Wells isn't a man to give up. Wouldn't surprise me if he's got men scouring these mountains looking for us right now. They might come across this canyon any time. Keep that in mind while I'm gone."

"Where're you going?" Kell asked.

"To Prentiss. I want to talk to Richard Courtney. I intend to authorize him to make loans to any honest settler looking for a place to farm or ranch as long as he stays within fifty miles of Prentiss. But they must be men who are willing to fight for the land they settle on."

Phil chuckled. "That'll take in most of the range Evan Wells claims."

"Exactly," Walt said.

Walt, fearing Cougar might be recognized, caught the grulla and saddled him, slipping out of the canyon at midnight, having already discussed his leaving with Kell and Phil. When he rode into Prentiss a few days later, he made sure he arrived at night, taking back alleys until, eventually, he pulled up before Richard Courtney's home, the most expensive place in Prentiss.

Leaving the dun tied at the hitchrack, Walt walked up the flower-bordered walkway, stepped up onto the spacious front porch, and knocked. Getting no response, he knocked again, harder this time.

"Who is it?" Richard Courtney called from within.

"An emergency!" Walt yelled. "I need to talk with you!"

A moment later, the door was opened slightly, and Richard Courtney peered through the crack. Walt gave the door a firm push, brushing Courtney back, and stepped inside.

"Sorry to do that," Walt apologized. "Do you remember me?"

"Mr. Davis, what're you doing in Prentiss? Don't you know you're a wanted man? Evan Wells has put a price on your head."

"That doesn't surprise me," Walt replied, "but I've got business with you."

"If drawing your money from my bank is your business, you'll have to wait till morning."

"I don't want to withdraw my money," Walt said. "In fact, in a few days I might want to deposit that much or more."

"That much and more? You mean more gold?" asked Courtney.

"Yes."

"You've made a strike somewhere," Courtney said. "You wouldn't want to let your banker in on the location, I guess."

"Wouldn't be worth your while, Mr. Courtney," Walt replied. "I've scraped the bottom of the barrel. There's not a flake left. But there's something else I want to talk to you about."

"Sit down," Courtney said, pointing to a silk-covered divan, while the banker sat in a chair opposite. "I'm listening," Courtney said, watching Walt intently.

"I want you to fix up a paper, which I'll sign, authorizing you to loan out my money," Walt began. "Then I want you to make loans to any worthy settler who wishes to file on land within a fifty-mile radius of Prentiss. The mortgage papers will contain the usual with one added clause. That clause will read that the borrower will forfeit his mortgage if he fails to lend assistance to any settler who is threatened by another rancher, regardless of who that rancher is."

"Of course, you really mean Evan Wells," Courtney said.

"I do."

Courtney was silent for a moment, thinking. "You'll tear this county apart," he said. "If you do this, you'll be fomenting a range war."

"Not if Evan Wells leaves his neighbors alone," Walt replied. "How long will it take you to draw up a paper giving you that authority?"

"A matter of minutes."

"Then get to it, and I'll wait to sign it."

"You haven't asked me about the widow Barry and Maudie," the banker said as he wrote out the document.

"How're they doing?" asked Walt.

"The daughter, Maudie, started performing in the

Golden Bucket. She took up with Jonas Pascal. Mrs. Barry is doing very well. Along with the laundry, she's begun to take in boarders. I guess Pascal thought Maudie and her mother had come into a whole passel of money. Pascal talked Maudie into showing him where her mother kept it. He took it and the two ran off together. That was three weeks ago. They haven't been heard from since."

"How much money did Pascal get?" asked Walt.

"Mrs. Barry couldn't say to the penny, but she guessed about five hundred dollars."

"Too bad she didn't keep her money in your bank," Walt observed.

"I told her as much, but I guess she doesn't trust banks. That five hundred dollars won't last Pascal long. Then he'll drop Maudie like a hot brick. I just hope she has the sense to come home when it happens, but you never know about women."

"Does Mrs. Barry need more?" asked Walt.

"I asked her, and she vows she'll get by. I believe her. She's a frugal lady."

"You keep an eye out for her," Walt said. "See to it she has what she needs to get by."

"If you say so."

"I do, and now I'd better get out of here," Walt said. "I need to be far gone when the sun comes up."

"Where're you going?" asked Courtney. "Mind telling me in case I need to get in touch with you?"

"Best I keep that to myself," Walt said, "but I'll be checking in from time to time. Now, would you mind dousing that lamp while I slip out?"

Courtney did so, and Walt, opening the door, stepped into the darkness. He was nearing the hitchrack when he saw movement near the grulla. Pulling up, he watched a small figure come from the darkness and begin to pull at the strap which fastened a saddlebag. Nothing but a boy, Walt thought to himself, but still a thief. Tiptoeing forward, he grabbed an arm and held on firmly while the small figure fought savagely to get free.

"You might as well give up, kid," Walt warned. "I reckon if you don't, I'll have to tan your bottom. How would you like that?"

The struggle abruptly ceased, and Walt pulled the now compliant young thief into the dim light thrown from Courtney's window and looked into the thinnest, dirtiest face he'd ever seen. The boy was dressed in rags hardly recognizable as clothes, and he was barefoot. Walt's heart went out to him.

"You oughtn't be stealing, son," he said. "Plenty of folks in town would feed you if you ask."

"They'd feed me," the boy said, "then they'd stick me back in that derned orphanage. I already run away from there twice. That preacher beats me, and I ain't going back!"

Walt remembered the Reverend Thomas Pickering who ran the orphanage. The man's face had the bluish tint of skimmed milk and the expression of a man who'd just eaten a green persimmon. Walt hadn't known the reverend well, but the few times he'd been around Pickering, Walt's impression was that every drop of compassion had been squeezed from the man's heart. Maybe something should be done about Pickering. He'd have to give some thought to the matter.

"How old are you?" Walt asked.

"I don't rightly know, sir."

"You got any folks?"

"No, sir."

"What happened to them?"

"Ma died of the fever. After that, Pa drank himself to death."

"What's your name?"

"Tony. Tony Haskell."

Walt was silent for a moment. He was envisioning the boy turned loose in the canyon. There would be horses to ride and fish to catch. A perfect place for a boy to grow up, and Connie and Misty could also give him some schooling from Hank Green's books which were still in the cave.

"Are you willing to do as grownups tell you?" Walt asked.

"Depends on what they tell me," the boy replied.

"Nothing bad, but I know a place you'd like, and some folks who'd be good to you. You could ride horses, and there's a lake full of fish. I'd like to take you there, but I have to know you'd behave and mind the grownups till you're a few years older."

"This place ain't no orphanage, is it?" Tony asked.

"Far from it. How about it? Would you like to go?"

"Will you be there?"

"If I ever leave for good, I'll take you with me . . . if you want to go, that is. How about it?"

"You got anything to eat while we're riding?" Tony asked.

Reaching into the saddlebag the boy had opened, Walt took out a couple of sticks of jerky. "Chew on that," he said. Stepping into the dun's saddle, he gave the boy a lift up behind him.

We gotta give you a bath, boy, the first stream we come to, Walt thought to himself, *but before we do that we gotta get you some decent clothes.* He touched his heels to the dun's side and sent the big horse along the street. When he came to the mercantile, he entered an alley and pulled up in front of the back door.

He gave Tony the dun's reins. "Reckon you can take care of him for maybe five minutes?" he asked Tony.

"I reckon, but where're you going?"

"To get you some clothes. I'll be back soon."

"What if someone comes along and wants to know what I'm doing here on this hoss?"

"Tell 'em I paid you to look after him," Walt said. "That satisfy you?"

"I reckon."

Walt walked to the back of the mercantile and put a shoulder against the door, giving it a hard push. The door gave but didn't open. A harder push and the lock gave way, allowing the door to swing inward. Walt had been in the store many times and knew where the clothes were.

When he reached the counter, he risked striking a match. Locating the shelf marked boys, he examined the clothes briefly. Then he selected two pairs of denim pants, a couple of work shirts, some socks, underwear, and a small, flat-crowned, wide-brimmed hat, similar to the one he wore. The boot rack was nearby, and he chose a pair he thought would fit the boy loosely, giving his feet a little room to grow. On his way past the cash register counter, he left a fifty dollar bill in plain sight, more than enough to pay for what he had taken.

He hoped he'd never regret what he was doing, and no man could read the future, but he liked and respected Tony's grit, and any youngster needed decent clothes, a home, and someone to look out for him.

When he was outside again, he gave the bundle to Tony. "Reckon you can hold on to them?"

"What is it?"

"Some clothes for you."

"Can't I put them on?"

"Not till we find a place where you can take a bath."

"Ah, shucks! A bath? I hate taking baths!"

"I know," Walt said and laughed.

Chapter Nineteen

Walt turned the grulla toward the mountains and this time, with no pursuit and carrying double, let the horse set his own pace. The sun rose behind them a few hours later. The purplish line of foothills could barely be seen in the distance, but the rising sun painted them a dull crimson. Recognizing the cottonwoods that surrounded the limestone sink hole where he'd camped with the others on his last trip into the mountains, Walt turned the grulla in, passed through the trees, and pulled up before the spring.

Walt let the boy down first and then swung to the ground himself. He let the dun drink while he filled his canteen. "Time for that bath I promised you," he said to Tony.

"Do I have to?" Tony asked.

"If you want to wear your new clothes."

"All right," Tony acquiesced, "but it's asking a lot." Slipping out of the ragged garments, he waded into the water. "This water is dadgummed cold," he said and shivered.

Walt took a used bar of soap from the grulla's saddle-bag and slipped off his own boots and socks. Rolling up his sleeves, he took a couple of steps into the shallow pool. Then he reached a foot out and tripped Tony, sending him splashing backward to the bottom of the pool. When Walt pulled him up, Tony was so angry he hopped up and down, sputtering and spitting. "Dadgum you, mister!" he shouted as he swiped at his face and eyes. "Dadgum you all the way to hell!"

"You cut out that kind of talk," Walt started to warn, but the sight was too much for him, and he burst into laughter. A mistake, because the next instant he felt a pair of small arms wrap about his knees. He was given a shove that sent him sprawling face first into the water. When he rolled over and looked up, he found Tony standing over him, his face filled with a mixture of anger and glee.

"Darned if this water isn't a little cold," Walt said as casually as he could muster. "Now that I'm wet, reckon I might as well take a bath myself."

Washed clean from head to toe and dressed in his new clothes, the hat set firmly on his head, Tony Haskell looked like a different boy. He seemed like a different person too as he stared at his reflection in the pool.

"Thanks, Mr. Davis," he said, turning to Walt, "and I'm sorry I dunked you."

"Guess I needed a bath too," Walt replied and laughed. "Anyway, we're buddies. You can call me Walt. Could you scare up some firewood before it gets any darker?" Walt asked.

"Reckon so," Tony said and scooted away.

"Look out for rattlers!" Walt called after him.

Walt relieved the grulla of his gear, offered him water again, and then staked him out on some thin grass. Next, he took a frying pan and bacon from his supply bag. Tony had returned by the time Walt had sliced several strips of bacon into the pan.

"Reckon you can get a fire going?" he asked the boy.

"If you've got some matches," Tony replied.

Reaching into his supply bag again, Walt tossed him a match tin and watched Tony gather a handful of dry grass, pile a few dry twigs on that, and add some of the larger sticks he'd brought in. Then he stuck a lighted match to the grass. The flame caught and began to build.

"You've done that before," Walt said.

"I had to sleep out a lot."

He's led a pretty bleak life, Walt thought to himself as he rolled a couple of stones to either side of the fire. His thoughts went to the other kids under Pickering's care. There had to be something he could do to improve their lot.

He filled the coffeepot with water and set it next to the fire to boil. Setting his frying pan on the stones, he let the fire lick at the bottom, and soon the bacon began to sizzle. The water had begun to boil, and he emptied a half cup of grounds into the pot. Soon, the smell of sizzling bacon and boiling coffee drifted through the trees.

When the bacon was almost crisp, he emptied a can of beans over the meat. When the beans were hot, he set the skillet aside and took two tin plates from the supply bag. He served a generous portion on the first and passed it to Tony, who had hardly taken his eyes from the skillet after the food had begun to cook.

"Eat," Walt ordered.

He served his own plate and filled two cups with coffee, passing one to Tony. Despite his hunger, the boy ate with a disciplined restraint, and Walt wondered where he'd picked it up. "Eat up," he urged. "There's another plateful waiting when you finish that."

When the meal was over, Tony, who could barely keep his eyes open, offered to clean the dishes.

"I'll take care of that chore in a moment," Walt said. Going to his saddle, he took his bedroll and spread it out. "Crawl in here, Tony," he told the boy.

"But where will you sleep?"

"Never mind about me," Walt replied. "This'll be your bed for tonight."

Tony, too tired and sleepy to resist, did as he was told. He was already asleep by the time Walt tucked the blankets snugly about him. Walt knelt beside him for a moment and listened to his even breathing. Then, taking the grulla's saddle blanket, he wrapped the blanket about himself and sat with his back to the trunk of a cottonwood. The blanket smelled richly of the grulla, a familiar smell, and not a bad smell to a man who depended on a horse for his living and often for his life.

Buster Alison gradually became aware of the clink of iron on rock as he sat in the temporary camp with a cup of coffee in his hand. Recognizing the sound, he quickly set the cup aside and, rising, got to the gray gelding just in time to cover its snout before the animal could offer a welcoming whinny. Leading the horse deeper into the brush, he waited. A few moments later, the rider appeared, two riders actually, a man and a boy on a big grulla horse.

As he studied the man, he was amazed to see that the description he'd been given of Walt Davis fit the man on the grulla in every detail from the rangy build to the thick shoulders, brown hair with bleached ends, and even the flat-crowned, wide-brimmed, black hat atop his head.

"That's my man, sure as Satan," Alison muttered. "This is going to be easy." Though he was fairly certain the man was Davis, the fact that he might be mistaken didn't bother Alison. When the man and boy were dead, he'd check the man's pockets and make sure.

Their present course would bring them within fifty feet of where Alison was hiding, a perfect shot for the Mills .75. Alison drew the gun and waited. As the horse and riders drew near, he took careful aim. Just as he squeezed the trigger, the grulla horse caught the scent of Alison's gray and gave a soft whinny, took a quick step, and threw up his head. The move was just enough to throw Alison's aim off. Still, he heard a loud grunt of pain as the grulla gave a long leap forward and rounded a copse of trees, giving Alison no chance for a second shot.

He climbed aboard the gray, eased the horse from the brush, and rode in the general direction taken by the fleeing party. The trail led upward and was easy to follow for the first half mile or so. Then it disappeared completely and, try as he might, Alison failed to find it again.

"He ain't dead, and he's a smart one," Alison muttered.

The possibility that he might be ambushed himself was in Alison's mind, and he watched the gray and his pack pony for any indication that either caught a whiff of another horse. Mountain-bred and raised wild before he was caught and tamed, the gray could sniff another horse a quarter mile off. After a few miles of climbing and no attack, Alison ceased to worry. Apparently, Davis was intent on making his escape rather than stopping to fight.

So intent was Alison on the trail that he would have sent the gray over the edge and into the canyon had the horse not balked. "Could have killed us both," muttered Alison gratefully to the gray, peering into the depths that had opened up before him.

He caught the scent of smoke and, casing the canyon, saw two women busy around a cooking fire. "Got to be where Davis and his outfit disappeared to," he muttered, "and Davis may have beat me here and be down there already." As he studied the women, he saw that both were fairly young, but one looked to be hardly out of her teens. "Just about the purttiest thing I ever saw," he muttered. "Reckon I won't kill her . . . not right off anyways."

* * *

"Are you hurt bad?" asked Tony when Walt pulled up and slipped to the ground.

"I don't think so, but it stings like the devil," Walt replied.

"Where'd you get hit?"

"In my left shoulder."

"You want I should bandage it for you?" Tony asked. "Might help stop the bleeding, but I ain't got nothing for a bandage."

"We'll use my shirttail," Walt said, "but we need some hot water. Reckon you could whip up a fire right quick?"

"Sure."

"Put the fire beneath that cedar," Walt said, pointing to the tree. "It'll filter and scatter the smoke. Maybe whoever shot at us won't see it."

While Tony got the fire going, Walt shed his shirt and, using his knife, cut two narrow strips from the tail and gave them to Tony. "Wet one and use it to clean the wound," he told the boy. Remembering the Indian remedy he used on Phil, he looked around for a prickly pear, but found none.

The bullet had cut a gash in the fleshy part of the shoulder a half inch deep. Walt was amazed at Tony's treatment of the wound, and how sympathetic he was of Walt's pain. At the same time, he was as businesslike and detached as a doctor. "We need something to stop the bleeding," Tony said when he had finished cleaning the wound.

"Look around and see if you can find a spider's web," Walt told him.

"A spider's web? What for?"

"Just find one, and I'll show you," Walt replied.

Circling, Tony began his search, returning a few moments later with a small wad of web. "Found it in a hollow log," he said to Walt.

Walt took the web and carefully spread it out, and

stretched it over the gash. Within seconds, the wound had ceased to bleed.

"Reckon you'll remember that," Walt asked, indicating his shoulder, "if you ever need to stop a wound from bleeding again?"

"I'll remember," Tony replied.

"Now see how snug you can wrap it with those strips," Walt said.

"You reckon you'll be able to ride?" asked Tony as he worked at the bandage.

"Well, we got a fire going already," Walt replied. "Why don't we stay the night here. You think you could make us some coffee and cook up some beans for supper?"

"Sure," replied Tony. "Who tried to ambush us, Walt?"

"I told you about my trouble with the W–in–a–Box and Evan Wells," Walt replied. "His men have been searching for me. Must have been one of them."

"Reckon they'll find us here?"

"Not before morning if we put out the fire before dark."

"How am I gonna clean the dishes without water?" Tony asked when they had finished eating.

"Scrub them out with sand," Walt suggested. "Then wipe them clean."

"You got a remedy for just about everything," Tony said when he was finished with the dishes.

"Not everything," Walt replied, but teaching the boy things did give him pleasure, Walt thought to himself. "Now spread that bedroll and crawl in," he continued. "You've had a rough day."

"I'll spread the blankets, but I ain't the one who's wounded. You can sleep in them tonight, and I'll use the horse blanket."

Seeing the serious look on the boy's face, Walt didn't object. "Are you gonna turn in?" Walt asked.

"Directly," replied Tony.

"Be sure the fire is out before you do."

"All right."

Walt dozed off despite the wound. Sometime later he awoke, raised himself, and looked around. Tony sat with the horse blanket about his shoulders, his chin resting on his chest as he slept. Even in sleep he held Walt's rifle across his lap.

Walt's heart suddenly swelled with love for the boy. The emotion was the most intense he'd felt since his mother died. Was this the way a father felt when he looked at his son?

Chapter Twenty

Keeping out of sight, but in a position that allowed him to see the entire canyon, Alison watched the women prepare supper and then call the two men in to eat, neither of whom appeared to be Walt Davis, nor did he see the boy. "I musta got him," he muttered, "but I'll make sure when I go down and get the woman." He had made a careful study of the canyon and had seen the ledge that led down to the bottom, and he had made up his mind not to leave the mountains without her.

Alison watched as the four finished eating. By then, the sun was setting, streaking the western sky with gold and red. One of the men and the two women entered the cave near where the cooking had been done, while the other went to a cave a little further on.

The cooking fire died out as darkness closed in over the canyon, and for awhile Alison seemed to be staring into a dark pit. Then the stars came out, some so low as to seem to rest on the taller mountain peaks, and spread a silver light over everything. A near full moon drifted in from the northwest and sent its beams into the canyon. Even Buster

Alison, a man incapable of respect for anything, found himself gazing silently upon the spectacle.

He tied the gelding off to a bush near where the ledge led into the canyon and continued down on foot. He had made a mental note of the location of both caves and headed first for the one which held the lone man. He'd have to kill both men in order to make his escape with the girl. The other woman? He'd have to kill her too, or she might be able to identify him later. He had killed women before but, strangely, hadn't much stomach for it.

Alison stopped at the mouth of the cave and peered inside. He could hear a man breathing, but he couldn't make out his position despite the moonlight filtering into the cave. Unsheathing the knife at his belt, he eased forward, placing each foot down carefully, fearing he'd kick a loose stone. When he reached the sleeping figure, he went down on one knee, grabbed the man's hair, and sliced the knife across his throat. The man struggled for a moment, and then lay still. Alison struck a match and, as he'd figured, the man wasn't Davis. He wiped his knife blade on the man's blanket and left the cave.

He sheathed the knife and drew his gun when he approached the cave in which the women and the other man slept. Standing in the entrance for a moment, he decided he needed a light to keep from killing the younger woman by mistake. Stepping back, he grabbed a handful of grass, struck a match, and stuck it to the grass. He entered the cave, the torch in his left hand, his gun in his right.

"Kell, is that you?" asked the man who pushed himself up.

The torch lit the man's face, and Alison could see the man wasn't Davis, but that made no difference. Aiming at the man's chest, he squeezed the trigger. The force of the bullet threw the man backward, the explosion waking the women. Alison took enough time to distinguish between the two and then shot the older and larger woman.

"You ain't got nothing to worry about, sugar," he said to the younger woman. "Old Alison's got plans for you, but not before we get outta this place."

Alison almost had his hands on Misty before she could react. Then, in desperation, she came to life. Grabbing the rifle Phil always kept nearby, she scooted back into the cave as far as she could and, fired it blindly as she retreated.

The man let out a curse and flung himself forward before Misty could shoot again. Landing on top of her, he made a grab for her arms in an effort to pin them to her sides. He caught one arm, but the other remained free. Raising her free hand to Alison's face, Misty raked downward with her fingernails, ripping the intruder's eyes. Alison shouted a curse and, drawing back a fist, smacked her on the jaw, snapping Misty's head back against the rocky floor of the cave and knocking her out cold.

When Misty came to, her jaw ached from the blow. She felt the swaying motion associated with riding and caught the strong smell of saddle leather. She tried to move, and found she could only shift her hands and feet, and those only slightly. Opening her eyes, she found herself staring at Checkers' hoofs and legs, recognizing them because of the many times she'd groomed the horse. Twisting about to look ahead, she saw a man on a big gray horse who held Checkers' reins in his hand, leading the pony.

"Untie me and let me down!" she screamed at the man.

Pulling up, the man swung from the saddle, walked back, and peered down into Misty's face. "I see you've come around, sugar," he said, the sound of his voice and the endearment sickening to Misty.

"Untie me at once!" she ordered. "I need to sit up!"

"Reckon that wouldn't hurt," the man said, "but you make a move to get away and I'll smack you again."

"Who are you and where're you taking me?" Misty asked as she was being untied.

"The moniker is Buster Alison, sugar, and you're going to get to like me."

The smell of the man was almost overwhelming, and Misty tried desperately not to vomit as she sat upright in the saddle. At least she was free, she told herself, as Buster Alison returned to his own mount. Maybe she'd get a chance to escape.

Walt pulled up and looked down into the canyon. "That's your home for the time being," he said to Tony.

"How do we get down there?" asked the youngster.

"See that ledge going down over there?" Walt said and pointed.

"Yes, sir."

"That's the only way to get to the bottom and the only way out."

"I don't see any of the folks you were telling me about," Tony said.

"Neither do I," Walt replied, and a feeling that something was wrong suddenly rose within him. "Maybe we should get down there and check on them."

"I'll walk and you ride," Walt said when they reached the ledge. "But best you hold on tight in case the grulla gets a little nervous going down."

"Maybe I should walk too," Tony said, a little apprehensively.

"If you want to," Walt replied and waited for Tony to slide down. With Tony at his heels, he led the procession down the ledge.

There was no sign of anyone as they approached the caves. "The women must be up at the mine with the men," he said, reassuringly, "but you stay outside here a moment, Tony, just in case." Then Walt stepped inside and saw the bodies of Connie and Phil.

"Dear God, what's happened here?" he said, hardly believing what he saw.

"What is it?" asked Tony, entering.

"You wait outside!" Walt commanded, and for once the youngster didn't question the order.

Kneeling between the two bodies, Walt saw the bullet holes. Then, remembering Misty, he panicked. "Come with me!" he said to Tony as he came out and almost ran to the cave in which he and Kell had slept.

"Stay outside!" he again ordered Tony and, entering, saw Kell whose throat gaped open like a huge obscene mouth. He frantically searched the cave for Misty. Then the truth dawned on him. Whoever had done the killing had taken Misty with him.

Chapter Twenty-one

Walt puzzled over who might have done the killing as he buried his friends. The whole affair resembled something Evan Wells might have ordered, he decided, only bloodier than usual. But despite everything that had happened, he couldn't imagine even Evan Wells ordering women slaughtered.

Walt buried his three friends side by side, marking each grave with a large stone at the head. He spent another hour adding to his supplies from the cave in which he'd found Phil and Connie. Then he spent some time watering the horses, checking their saddles, and getting them ready for the ride. He was glad he hadn't had to push them too hard on the long trip from Prentiss.

As he went about the chores, he couldn't rid himself of the images of his brutally slaughtered friends. What kind of man would viciously slit a man's throat from side to side and then shoot down a woman? These were people he'd come to depend on, people he liked, and he vowed to revenge their deaths when he caught their killer. They were desperate thoughts, but they seemed to relieve a little of the awful fury that filled his mind.

He would have felt better had there been someone with whom to leave Tony, but he had no choice but to take the boy along. He was surprised, too, at the way his shoulder had scabbed over. He'd often heard that wounds healed faster in high altitudes, and he decided he had proof now that such was the case.

They had been in the canyon for three hours when they rode out again, Walt riding Cougar, Tony on the older, less rambunctious grulla, the spotted mare carrying the pack of supplies as well as the gold Phil and Kell had dug. Walt wondered how the killers had missed it.

Something else gave him hope. When they had roped the horses, Walt had missed Checkers, Misty's pony. Walt, familiar with the pony's hoof prints, was sure he'd recognize them if he came across them. *That might make the job of tracking down the killers a little less difficult*, he thought to himself.

They circled the canyon looking for tracks and soon picked up the trail, but instead of heading in the direction toward town, the trail went north, away from Prentiss and away from the W-in-a-Box. That puzzled Walt. He had expected the killers would head directly for the W-in-a-Box, as they had so often in the past.

"What's to the north?" Tony asked.

"A lot of wild country till you get out of Colorado," replied Walt. "Then there's Wyoming."

"Any towns?"

"Cheyenne and Laramie are the closest."

"You ever been there?" asked Tony.

"A couple of times," Walt replied.

Misty felt much better sitting astride, her hands and feet free of the ropes. She was determined to escape the clutches of the terrible, smelly man who had taken her, for there was no mistaking the lascivious look in his eyes each time he turned back and looked at her, as he did frequently. She couldn't keep from shuddering at what the look portended. Somehow she had to escape before he decided he'd gotten far enough away from the canyon to feel safe from pursuit.

That he was concerned about pursuit was obvious, for he often pulled up when topping a rise to study his back trail. She was puzzled by that, since he'd left no one alive who might have been able to follow them. But Misty drew comfort from the very fact that he was apprehensive. Maybe his concern that they might be followed would give her the chance to escape.

The sun was halfway down, still hot on the left side of her face, when the man turned into the small canyon that ran fifty yards back into the hills. A small grove of pine and juniper extended from the back wall. Green grass abounded, and Misty knew the canyon had water. Arriving among the trees, she saw the spring, a tiny stream that ran from beneath some rocks to form a small pool which overflowed and disappeared into the thirsty soil beneath the trees.

The man pulled up well within the trees and near the spring. Sliding from the gray, he untied a sack he carried behind his saddle and tossed it in Misty's direction.

"Get down and fix us some vittles," he ordered.

Misty hadn't eaten since the night before, so she was happy to oblige. "What's your name again?" she asked the man who had breasted himself down over the spring to drink and now sat with his back to a pine.

"Buster Alison," he replied, apparently pleased that she was interested enough to ask. "I reckon you must have heard of old Buster at one time or another."

"Why? Are you famous?"

"I reckon you could say that. People know old Buster from Montanny to Ole Mexico."

"I need a match," Misty told him when she had the tinder ready to light.

Alison ran a hand into a pocket, brought out a tin, and tossed it to her. As Misty lit the fire, he drew forth a sack of tobacco and rolled himself a smoke, lighting it when Misty returned the matches, his eyes never leaving the slim figure of Misty as she worked.

Misty found a frying pan, a coffeepot, a couple of tin plates and cups, a couple of spoons, coffee, a tin of beef, several cans of beans, and biscuits in the sack. Almost hidden at the bottom she discovered a can opener. She soon had coffee boiling and beans and beef cooking in the skillet. When they were hot, she filled a plate, poured a cup of coffee, and carried them to Alison, who still sat with his back to the pine.

"Why, thank you, sugar," he said and reached for the plate.

When the idea popped into Misty's head, she acted immediately. Turning the plate upside down, she emptied the plate of food in Alison's lap. Alison let out a scream, pushed himself up hurriedly, and began a sort of hopping dance about the campsite.

The horses stood maybe twenty feet from the camp wearily pulling at the grass. Misty made a sudden dash for Checkers, grabbed his rein along with that of the gray, and pulled herself into Checkers' saddle.

"Hey! Come back here!" she heard Alison yell as she sent Checkers in a run toward the exit of the canyon.

The gray, not anxious to run, held her back and nearly pulled her arm from the socket, but she held on to his rein despite the pain, though she was sure her arm would never be the same again. Then a gun exploded behind her, and she felt the hot breath of a bullet zip past her ear. Obviously, Alison had recovered from the hot food she'd dumped into his lap. Another explosion followed immediately and, lowering herself to Checkers' neck, she urged him on. The gray, frightened by the explosions, maybe even the snarl of the passing bullets, decided to run. She knew Alison would catch her if she let the gray go, for he would, no doubt, return to Alison.

"Go boy!" she shouted in Checkers' ear, and the pony responded with all the effort he could muster.

Reaching the exit of the canyon, she turned south and rode in the direction they'd come. From behind her came another shot and, turning in the saddle to look back, she saw Buster Alison. He'd made it out of the canyon and was running after her, but she was now too far for his handgun to be anywhere near accurate, and she knew the man's rifle still rode in the sock on the gray's saddle.

Only when Buster Alison was a tiny figure behind her did Misty allow Checkers to slow down, and only when he was out of sight for some time did she pull the pony up and slide from the saddle to give him a rest. She felt weak but exhilarated from the close escape. Her heart still racing and her breath short, she sank to the ground at Checkers' feet to rest.

She had never been this far north before, but she knew Prentiss had to be approximately thirty miles to the southeast. She was trying to decide whether she should follow the foothills south or cut back across the plains when she spotted the two riders coming toward her a half mile away. They looked to be following the trail she and Alison had put down.

Her first reaction was panic, and she looked around for a place to hide. Seeing no such place available, she rushed back to the gray and slipped Alison's rifle from the sack.

She had fired rifles before, but never one as large and as heavy as Alison's big buffalo gun. The barrel was thick and octagonal, and so heavy she had trouble lifting it. Dropping behind a boulder, she waited for the riders to come closer. They were still a couple of hundred yards away when she recognized Walt's horses and then Walt. The second rider was a boy she'd never seen before. Dropping the heavy rifle, she ran toward them, never so happy to see anyone in her life.

Walt spurred Cougar to a run. When he came alongside Misty, he pulled up and slid from the saddle. Misty threw herself into his arms and wrapped her arms about his neck and, with tears of relief, refused to let go. After a moment, Walt regretfully loosened her arms, but he would always remember the warmth of her body against his as she clung to him.

"Tell me what happened, Misty."

"A man slipped into the cave," she began. "Before we knew what was happening, he shot Connie and Phil. I grabbed Phil's gun and tried to fight back, but he knocked me out. We were out of the canyon and I was on Checkers when I came to. What about Kell?" she asked.

"Dead too," Walt replied grimly. "How did you manage to get away?"

"I caught him off guard and took the horses."

"Where is he?"

"Back there somewhere. He was coming after me when I lost sight of him." Stepping back from Walt, she looked up at Tony. "Where did you find this handsome fella?"

"Misty Wells, meet Tony Haskell," Walt said. "Tony lives with me now."

"Howdy, miss," Tony said and tipped his hat slightly. The grownup gesture brought a smile to Misty's face.

"May I say it's nice to meet a gentleman from time to time?" Misty made a slight curtsy.

Tony's face turned as red as a beet, and Walt turned quickly away to keep Tony from seeing his smile. "Will you do me a favor, Tony?" he asked when he had recovered.

"What?" the boy asked.

"I want you to stay here and look after Miss Wells while I see if I can find the man who tried to run off with her."

"I reckon I can do that," Tony replied.

Walt gave Misty a wink and climbed aboard Cougar.

Buster Alison saw the lone horseman's cautious approach. Assuming the rider had run into Misty Wells and was now on the lookout for him, Alison quickly took shelter behind a large boulder. "I could have picked him off from here," he muttered, "if I hadn't let that tricky female get away with my rifle."

He waited until the rider was within range of the Mills .75 and, cocking the pistol, took a good look at the man before he pulled the trigger. For a moment he was startled by his good fortune and muttered, "That's got to be Davis, and he ain't dead. Couldn't be another man answering the same description. Reckon I'll earn the rest of my money now after all," and he squeezed off a shot.

The bullet struck the rider's saddle horn and careened off into the distance, making a whining sound. Startled, the horse began to buck, throwing up a cloud of dust. Then, suddenly, the saddle was empty, and Alison thought he saw the man disappear into some shoulder-high sage that grew along the slight trail. He sent two shots into the sage, hoping to get lucky. The horse, frightened, galloped back the way he had come, and Alison, knowing that his Mills was empty, took a moment to reload.

"You're a yellow ambusher, Alison!" the man shouted. "You slaughtered some good people in that canyon! I intend to see you pay for it! Are you man enough to come out from behind that rock and meet me in the open, face–to–face?"

Alison could hardly believe his ears. He had faced a dozen men, most known as fast guns, and he was being challenged by a man he'd never heard of till a few days ago. He smiled to himself. He'd kill Davis, take his horse, and hunt the girl down. Maybe he'd give her a beating for dumping the hot food in his lap before he took his pleasure.

"You want a face-off? Is that it?" he shouted.

"That's it!" came the reply. "You got the nerve?"

"No, don't do it, Walt! He'll kill you!" someone yelled and, turning, Alison saw Misty and the boy. They had pulled their horses up a few yards back, out of range of Alison's pistol. Both held rifles pointed in the direction of the boulder behind which Alison crouched. Misty struggled with Alison's heavy Sharps, and Tony carried Kell's Winchester, which he had taken as his own before they left the canyon.

"You still want that face-off, Davis?" Alison yelled.

"I do!"

"Then tell your friends to back up out of rifle range. Then we'll step out at the same time!" Alison shouted.

"You heard him!" Walt called to Misty and Tony. "Ride back out of range."

Both hesitated a moment and then followed Walt's instructions, stopping maybe fifty yards back.

"You ready now?" Walt shouted.

"Ready!" came Alison's reply.

Both men stepped into the open simultaneously and faced each other. Buster Alison slowly lowered himself into a crouch, his hand hovering over the big Mills .75. Walt was ready when Alison's hand made a dive for the Mills. Then his mind went blank for what seemed a long moment, but was really only the briefest of instants. He felt the grip of the Peacemaker smooth against his palm as his thumb found the hammer. All the while, a voice inside his head kept saying: *Don't rush it! Take your time! Remember, it's the first hit that counts, not who shoots first.*

The explosion of the guns sounded as if simultaneous. Walt felt the hot rush of a bullet past his ear. Then he heard a groan from Buster Alison, saw him clutch his chest, and watched him slowly go down. When he heard the cheers from behind him, he turned and saw Misty and Tony send their mounts in his direction.

Sliding from their mounts, Misty and Tony approached Walt, who stood over the prone figure of Buster Alison.

"Who was he?" Walt asked.

"I think he was someone my uncle hired to track you down and kill you," replied Misty.

"I'm glad he's dead," Tony said, "but why would he kill everyone back in the canyon?" he asked.

"He was paid to do it," Walt replied.

"What're we gonna do with the body?" asked Tony.

"We'll take him into town and turn him over to the undertaker," Walt said.

"But what about Uncle Evan?" asked Misty.

"Maybe it's time the two of us met face–to–face," replied Walt, grimly.

Chapter Twenty-two

Walt, having taken side–by–side rooms in the Hotel Prentiss, left Tony in the care of Misty and walked the short distance along the street to the Golden Bucket Saloon. When one wanted news of what was happening, a saloon was the place to go. He was surprised at how empty the place was when he pushed through the swinging doors and walked to the bar.

"What'll you have?" Jake Bonner asked as he swiped at the bar with a damp rag.

"My usual," replied Walt.

Jake placed a bottle of sarsaparilla before Walt. "If that catches on around here," he said, indicating the bottle, "I'll be out of business."

"I doubt that'll happen, but you'll have fewer fights to break up and fewer chairs and tables to replace," Walt said and smiled.

"You hear about the homesteader meeting?" asked Jake Bonner.

"I just got into town," Walt replied.

"The Wells outfit pushed a herd of cattle through Chimney Valley on the way to market in Denver," Bonner

said. "Murray Landers had settled in the valley. The
W–in–a–Box were prepared to run the cattle over
Landers' crops. When Landers objected, Ace Hawley shot
and killed him. Landers' murder left a widow and a
ten–year–old boy. The homesteaders are really angry over
the killing. They've called a meeting at Landers' place
today."

Walt had ridden through Chimney Valley a couple of
times on the way to Denver himself. The valley was
named after a fifty-foot-tall spiral of rock that rose near
its center. Landers should have known what to expect
when he settled there, Walt decided. Now his death would
probably lead to a fight between the W–in–a–Box outfit
and the homesteaders.

Walt knew he was responsible, since his money had
been the means by which the homesteaders had settled the
land. And this fight was what he had wanted all along. He
knew he'd have to take a hand in the fighting, but did he
want to leave Misty and Tony alone with no one to protect
them? Abruptly leaving the bar, he went along the street
to the mercantile.

The store was empty except for Chess Stoddard, the
owner, who tossed a fly swatter aside and rose to meet
Walt. "What can I do for you?" Stoddard asked.

"I'm looking to buy a gun," replied Walt. "A small pistol for a lady."

"This way," Stoddard said and led the way deeper into
the store. He paused before a glassed–in counter that con-
tained various handguns. The rifles rested on racks
attached to the wall.

"How about this one?" asked Stoddard, sliding the
counter door open. Reaching in, he brought out a Smith
and Wesson .38 pocket model. "It's meant for close shooting, but has knock down power as well," Stoddard said.

Walt took the gun and examined it carefully. The pistol

was compact and light with a rosewood grip and was attractive if a gun could be called attractive.

"Would you like to try it out?" Stoddard asked.

"I think I would," replied Walt.

Stoddard reached for a box of cartridges, made sure he had the right caliber, and gave them to Walt. "Then load her up and follow me," he said and led the way to the back door, stopping just outside. "Use that," he said, indicating a target enclosed by several bales of hay.

Walt took aim and squeezed off six quick shots.

"That's good shooting," Stoddard said, admiring the several holes within the center circle of the target.

Walt looked the gun over again. The recoil was slight and the gun was quite manageable for a woman. "I'll take it," he said. He thought of buying a rifle for Tony, but recalled that the boy had appropriated Kell's Winchester. Tony would prefer Kell's rifle over a new one any day.

Walt followed Stoddard back inside. "I'll need a holster for the pistol," he said. "You got anything in stock?"

"No new ones, but I do have a used one that'll do for the pistol," Stoddard said. "The holster's still on a cartridge belt. Maybe you'd like the belt as well?"

"Maybe, let's have a look."

Stoddard produced a belt and holster and passed them over for Walt's inspection. Both belt and holster had obviously been used, but only slightly, and both had been well oiled.

"Looks to have been used by a woman," Walt said, noting the length of the belt.

"A boy," replied Stoddard, "the Marsden boy. His pa bought him a bigger gun and holster last week."

"I'll take the pistol as well as the holster and belt," Walt said.

"Anything else I can show you?" Stoddard asked.

"No, but will you stand behind the pistol?" Walt asked.

"Absolutely. All my guns are tested before I buy them, but if anything wrong turns up, all you have to do is bring the gun back in. I'll make it good."

"That's good to know."

"Now about cartridges?" he asked.

"A couple of boxes," Walt told him. "And there is something else I need to talk to you about."

"What's that?"

"Did you find a fifty dollar bill on your counter one morning sometime back?"

"I did, and I found some merchandise missing as well."

"Did the fifty dollars take care of what was missing?"

"That and a good deal more," Stoddard said. "Why, do you know something about it?"

"I was the one who broke in," Walt admitted. "I had just picked up my boy, and he needed clothes."

"Well, that clears up a mystery."

"I hope you don't bear me a grudge," Walt said.

"Bear a grudge?" Stoddard asked. "Not likely, when you left enough money behind to pay more than double for what you took. You can break in my store anytime. Just leave me a note telling me it was you next time."

"I will," Walt said and, taking his purchases, left the mercantile, Stoddard following him all the way to the door.

Once back at the hotel, Walt climbed the stairs and knocked on Misty's door. Misty opened the door and invited Walt in.

"I find I have to go out of town," he said to Misty. "Would you mind looking after Tony for me?"

"Looking out for Tony would be my pleasure," Misty replied. "How long will you be gone?"

"I can't say exactly. A few days."

"Don't worry about Tony," Misty said. "He'll be fine with me. We can continue his lessons."

Walt was surprised Tony made no objections, though he had begun to see that the boy and Misty got along well together. He had also been pleased by Tony's increased interest in the books Misty had him reading. A boy needed the civilizing touch of a good woman, he thought to himself.

"I picked this up just in case," Walt said, offering the pistol and holster to Misty. "And you've still got Kell's rifle, haven't you, Tony?"

"Yes, sir. Would you like to see it?"

"He's been cleaning that gun for the past half hour," Misty said.

"Good, but be sure to keep it unloaded when you're inside. When I get back, I'll take you both out for some target practice," he added.

"You really think we need guns here in town?" Misty asked.

"I hope not, but you never know for sure," Walt replied. "Anyway, keep them handy just in case."

He left a couple of twenty dollar bills on a table. "If this runs out, go to Richard Courtney and get more. I have to stop by the bank before I go, and I'll tell him to expect you."

He was surprised when Misty suddenly crossed the room to where he stood. Standing on tiptoe, she rested her lips against his cheek. "Thanks for everything," she said.

Walt was too surprised to respond. Turning about, he passed through the door connecting the rooms and, hefting the bag of nuggets to his shoulder, stepped into the hallway and headed for the bank.

Richard Courtney had a customer at his desk when Walt entered the bank. But spying Walt, he was instantly on his feet and met Walt before he was through the door.

"Someone here who has been wanting to meet you," Courtney said, and led Walt to his desk where the stranger waited.

"Mr. Walt Davis, let me introduce Mr. Mack Hamilton," Courtney said. "Walt, Mack is one of the first homesteaders I approved for a loan. He's come in to make a payment."

Hamilton rose, and he and Walt shook.

"Mack and I have finished our business," Courtney said. "Now what can I do for you?"

Walt placed the bag of nuggets on the table. "Weigh these out, give me a receipt, and have them assayed," he said. "I'll take Mr. Hamilton out for a drink and a talk while you get that done."

Hefting the bag, Courtney hurried away.

Walt led Hamilton outside and down the block to the Golden Bucket. "Tell me about this business in Chimney Valley," Walt said when they were seated and had a drink before them, Walt a sarsaparilla, Hamilton a glass of rye.

Hamilton was a man of average height but well muscled in arms and shoulders, the kind of muscles a farmer develops from the heavy lifting encountered on a farm. Keen, intelligent blue eyes stared out of a sunburnt face at Walt.

"Not much to tell," Hamilton began, "other than Ace Hawley killed Murray Landers when Murray objected to the W–in–a–Box running a herd over his crops. The homesteaders are meeting at Landers' place now. I was running late on my loan payment and had to come into town, but I'm riding to Landers' place to join them now that I'm finished here."

"Mind if I ride along?" asked Walt.

"Not at all."

After talking the trouble over and finishing their drinks, the two returned to the bank where they found Courtney. "Don't have the results of the assay yet," Courtney told Walt. "Be some time yet."

"Deposit whatever the gold comes to in my account,"

Walt replied. "I'll be in to pick up the deposit receipt the next time I'm in town."

Walt and Hamilton left the bank, followed closely to the door by Courtney. The banker was obviously impressed by Walt's growing wealth. By almost any standard, Walt Davis was becoming a fairly wealthy man.

When Hamilton and Walt arrived at Landers' place, they found twenty or more angry men milling around before the Landers' cabin. Sarah Landers, dressed in black, sat in a rocker on the porch. The Landers' boy was perched on a stool nearby. The fear in the boy's eyes reminded Walt of the fear he'd seen in Tony's eyes the night Walt had caught him trying to steal.

The neighbor women were serving coffee and sliced beef between chucks of bread. Even they stopped when Walt and Hamilton rode in.

"We've been waiting for you, Mack," a burly rancher shouted as Hamilton and Walt slid from their mounts.

"Well, I'm here now," Hamilton replied, "and I've brought a man along we're all indebted to. Folks, I'd like you to meet Walt Davis."

A chorus of greetings met Hamilton's announcement. Several men stepped forward to shake Walt's hand and thank him for the loans. Others, unable to get near, shouted their thanks.

Walt stepped up on the cabin porch and raised his hands for silence. "I hope you've thought seriously about what will be in store for you if you attack the W–in–a–Box!" he said. "Evan Wells has twenty or more gunmen. Most have fought in range wars before. The attack will be no secret. All of Prentiss is aware of what you're about to do. The word will have reached the W–in–a–Box by now. They'll be waiting when you ride in. Most of you have families. Think of what they'll do without you, because some of you won't be coming back alive."

"What're you suggesting?" someone shouted. "That we let Murray's murderers go?"

"That's not what I'm suggesting at all," Walt replied. "What I'm saying is that you should have some sort of plan in mind. If you just ride in shooting, they'll knock half of you from the saddle on the first sweep."

Sudden quiet settled over the men as they considered Walt's words.

"You got something in mind?" someone asked.

"Maybe one or two suggestions," Walt replied.

"Then spit 'em out," a man called from the rear of the group rapidly gathering around Walt.

"Why don't we surround the W–in–a–B," Walt began. "Then someone can ride in and demand that Wells surrender Ace Hawley to us. If he does, we'll take Hawley to Denver and charge him with the murder of Landers. With Hawley out of the way, we'll have taken the starch out of Evan Wells and the rest of his men."

"What if Wells refuses to turn Hawley over?" Mack Hamilton asked.

"Then we'll take him, or have a go at it," Walt said.

There was silence for a moment as the men thought the suggestion over.

"Let's give it a try!" someone shouted.

"It's your idea, Davis!" someone else yelled. "You take charge and lead us!"

The riders topped a rise and pulled up to study the W–in–a–Box. The ranch was an impressive group of buildings. The large southern-style house set on a high knoll was surrounded by several red oaks. A slope ran down to a huge barn surrounded by several corrals. The bunkhouse, a long rectangular building, sat about halfway between the barn and the house.

There was little movement about the place, and Walt

found that strange for the headquarters of one of the biggest ranches in Colorado. That stillness suggested to him he had been right in his warning to the homesteaders. The W–in–a–Box crew was waiting for them. They would open up as soon as the homesteaders were within rifle range.

"Mack, you take half of the men and circle left, but before you go, suggest someone to lead the rest of the men who'll take up position to the right."

"Patrick Sneeds is a good man," Hamilton said.

Sneeds was a man whose age was hard to judge, but he was impressive in a quiet sort of way. His sunburnt, wrinkled face and eyes were those of a man who had maybe seen too much of a world he didn't particularly like. The only thing Walt knew about him was that he lived alone on his hundred and sixty acres, and Walt remembered Courtney talking about the improvements Sneeds had already made on his homestead.

"Mr. Sneeds, you take the other half and circle the place to the right and take up positions." He turned to the full group. "Men, I want you to remain in clear sight when you're in position, but stay out of rifle range. And this is important. There will be no firing till I give you some kind of signal. If there is, you're apt to get me killed."

"What're you planning to do?" asked Mack Hamilton.

"I'm going to ride down and parley," replied Walt. "I'll call Wells out and make him our offer . . . Ace Hawley, or we'll attack. If he refuses to give Hawley up, I'll turn around and ride out."

"And likely get shot in the back," Mack Hamilton remarked.

"No, I don't think so," Walt said, "not with all of you in plain sight and watching. Mack, Patrick, take your groups and get under way. Everyone stay alert to what's happening. No telling how this is going to pan out. Just be careful and try not to get yourselves killed."

Sneeds and Hamilton led out and the men, breaking into halves, followed them silently, the only sounds the creak of saddle leather and the occasional snort of a horse.

The house looked bigger and grander to Walt as he got closer. The front door was flanked by double windows, and several rocking chairs painted bright green graced a porch that stretched the width of the house. The house was made of squared logs, and here and there the white paint had peeled. The placed looked strong and substantial. Someone had put a lot of effort into the building, he decided.

A slight wind teased the leaves of the red oaks, and a squirrel scooted along the ground, a nut in his mouth, and raced up the trunk of the nearest oak. A blue tick hound came from beneath the steps, threw his head up, and barked sonorously a couple of times, causing Cougar to lower his head and snort threateningly. Walt pulled up and waited. No one came from the house, and the other buildings were also silent and seemingly vacant. Nevertheless, Walt had the feeling a dozen or so guns were trained on him.

"Hello!" he called.

A long, almost eerie silence followed. Then Brock Thurston, the foreman, came from the house, stopped on the front porch, and studied Walt a moment. "What do you want, Davis?" he asked, his voice and manner suggesting Walt's presence was barely tolerated.

"I came to talk to Mr. Wells," Walt replied.

"I'm afraid you're too late for that," Thurston said. "He's dead. Ace brought him in yesterday, said the old man was ambushed not too far from your place. Ace figures he went to talk to you about something, maybe to make a final offer on your place. You must have refused and killed him. Pretty cute you showing up here and asking to see him."

"Ace Hawley is wrong," Walt replied, "and so are you if you believe him. You'll have to find yourself another killer. Where is Hawley?"

"Ace and a couple of the boys have ridden into Prentiss to swear out a warrant for you. Boys!" Thurston called.

A couple of cowhands Walt had seen in Prentiss from time to time came from the house, six-guns drawn. They appeared ready to shoot at the slightest move from Walt.

"Get his gun, Martin," Thurston ordered.

"I'd hold up on that if I were you," Walt said.

"But I ain't you," Thurston replied. "Get his gun, Martin."

Walt knew that now the W–in–a–Box crew looked upon him as a mortal enemy with a price on his head. Once in their power, his life would very likely be forfeit. He waited until the man called Martin was between him and the other two men on the porch. Then, at just the right moment, he sank his spurs into Cougar's sides and simultaneously drew his six-gun. Cougar, unused to such treatment, lunged forward, knocking Martin to the ground.

At the same time, Walt turned the gun on the men on the porch. The first bullet caught Thurston in the leg, and the foreman let out a shout of pain and began hopping about on one leg, cursing with every hop. Whirling Cougar about, Walt threw himself forward in the saddle and rode for all he was worth for safety as bullets from a half dozen guns whizzed past his head. Then the guns of the homesteaders opened up, pouring lead from every direction down on the W–in–a–Box crew, chasing them back into the buildings from which they had just emerged.

When Walt was out of range, he pulled up, and

Hamilton rode out to meet him. "Liked to have got your-self killed," he said, a grim smile playing across his face.

"I don't think I was ever closer," Walt replied.

"You satisfied we got no choice but to fight them now?" Hamilton asked.

"I'm not sure Hawley is among them," replied Walt, "but the only way we're gonna know is to root them out. Thurston said Wells was ambushed near my place. They think I killed him. He said Hawley had ridden into town to swear out a warrant for my arrest, but that may be a bunch of crap just to muddy the water. We won't know for sure until we see who's inside there. Pass the word for the men to close in, and remind them to be careful. We don't want any dead heroes."

The homesteaders began their attack. Gradually moving in, they poured lead into every building, receiving a withering fire in return. A contingent reached the barn first, and a half dozen W–in–a–Box riders were flushed out and picked off as they raced for the bunkhouse. Someone set fire to the hay in the barn loft, and a moment later, red tongues of flame licked upward from the loft's door. Soon the fire had burned through the roof. Horses milled uneasily in the big corral as the heat increased.

Walt, maybe forty yards before the ranch, saw the danger to the horses. He wondered for a moment if they would break through the poles of the corral. Then he decided to take no chances and made a dash for the corral gate. Someone from the house spotted him and peppered the ground about him with bullets, some close enough to sprinkle him with dirt. Fortunately, smoke from the fire blossomed out to cover him.

He reached the corral gate and swung it open. Seeing a way to escape the rising heat and flames, the horses nearest the gate stampeded through in a squeeze so tight the gateposts gave way, and the small herd galloped through the ranch yard, heading for the distant mountains.

As if mesmerized by the stampeding herd, the guns suddenly went silent. A moment later what was left of the W–in–a–Box crew came from the remaining buildings, led by a limping Brock Thurston.

Walt stepped into the clear and covered them with his six-gun. "Unbuckle your gunbelts and let 'em drop," he ordered. "Then get busy and help keep the rest of these buildings from burning."

"Let 'em burn!" a homesteader yelled. "They burned ours to the ground!"

"So they did," Walt said, "but Evan Wells won't be running the W–in–a–Box after this. Men, some of you help contain the fire. The rest of you see if there's anyone still hiding in the house."

Several riders hurried to carry out the search, while the rest joined the W–in–a–Box riders to keep the fire from spreading. A few minutes later, the searchers returned with Evan Wells and Ezra Dudley, the cook.

"I thought you said Wells was dead, Thurston!" Walt shouted at the foreman.

"I lied!" replied Thurston.

"He thought maybe we wouldn't search the house!" someone shouted.

"What's the meaning of this?" Evan Wells demanded and, at the same time, struggled free of the men who held him.

"String the old bastard up!" someone yelled.

"There'll be no hanging!" Walt barked and stepped between Wells and the crowd, covering the farmers with his six-gun.

"The fight's over, men, and we've won," Walt replied. "We'll take Wells into Prentiss and jail him till the district judge makes his next visit. Then he'll be tried for those murders you mention. Otherwise, we're just as bad as he is."

"He's right, men," Mack Hamilton said, stepping forward to stand beside Walt. "But there's one still missing." Turning to Wells, he asked, "Where is Ace Hawley?"

"I'll tell you nothing!" Wells retorted disdainfully, too proud to answer any question put to him by a bunch he considered beneath him.

"Spread out and search some more," Walt told the circle of homesteaders. "Remember, he's dangerous. If you find him, call for help."

Ezra Dudley had remained quiet thus far. "Is Miss Misty all right?" he asked of Walt as the homesteaders dispersed.

"What's that to you?" Walt asked.

The old cook pulled himself erect, his eyes blazing. "That girl's a friend of mine," he said. "Who do you think fixed her all them late breakfasts since she come here? And who took her into town and got her away from here?"

"Why would you do that?" Walt asked.

"I liked that girl!" Ezra said, stepping forward to face Walt. "I was tired of seeing Ace Hawley sniffing around her!" Then the old cook turned on Evan Wells. "That girl was your niece," he growled, "your brother's daughter, the only kin you got left! Didn't you care what happened to her? Don't you care now?"

But Wells didn't wilt under the old cook's scorn. Instead, he merely turned his back and stared off into the distance.

"You're free to ride out, old timer," Walt said, addressing Ezra.

"What're you gonna do with the rest of the crew?" the old cook asked.

"Take 'em in with Mr. Wells, I reckon," replied Walt.

"Be a lot of trouble to you," Ezra said, "and there's some good men among them."

"You sound like you got a suggestion," Walt said.

"Well," Dudley drawled, "I'd turn 'em loose and let them ride out with the understanding that if they're ever caught again in Colorado, they'll be strung up from the nearest tree."

Walt turned to the homesteaders. "Men?" he asked.

There was silence for a moment. "Aw, let 'em ride out," someone drawled. "It's Wells and Hawley we want to see hang." The others agreed.

Walt turned to the remaining Wells riders. "You heard it, men. If you're ever seen in Colorado again, I'll help slip the noose around your neck myself." He indicated some of the horses that had begun to wander back in. "Get your gear, catch up some horses, and ride out of here. Better be quick about it before these men change their minds."

As the W–in–a–B riders rushed for the bunkhouse to gather their belongings, Walt took his rope from Cougar's saddle and caught up a horse for Wells. "You expect me to ride him bareback?" Wells demanded.

"Guess you have to," replied Walt. "I expect the fire got all the tack. Climb aboard."

"We've searched every nook and cranny," the homesteaders announced as they returned from their search, "and we can't find hide nor hair of Hawley."

"Maybe he lit out and is gone for good," Walt said. "Might be the best solution after all. Well, I'll get Wells into town and see he's locked up. What've the rest of you got in mind?"

"I ain't got no more business in Prentiss," Mack Hamilton said, "and Wells ain't gonna give you no trouble. Reckon I'll ride to my place and catch up on some work."

There was a chorus of agreement from the homesteaders, and they scattered for their horses.

Only Ezra Dudley remained. "What about you?" he asked the cook.

"Thought I'd ride in with you and see Miss Misty," the old man replied. "I reckon this place will belong to her now, and she'll need a good cook. Do you mind?"

"Be glad for the company," Walt told him.

Reaching for the lead rope for Wells' mount, Walt climbed aboard Cougar. When he was well out from the ranch, he turned and looked back at the silent buildings. The only movement about the place was a few spirals of smoke drifting up from the burned out barn.

Chapter Twenty-three

The sun had long since sunk behind the Rockies as Walt and Ezra approached Prentiss with the prisoner. Walt had ridden warily, for he had the idea that if Ace Hawley knew his boss had been taken prisoner, he might try to rescue him. But the trip was uneventful.

Except for the Golden Bucket and Riley's, the town was quiet with only a few lights casting squares along the street from the windows. Walt pulled up before the jail and swung down, ordering Wells to do the same.

"This place looks empty," Ezra remarked, sliding from the saddle.

"I imagine Marshal Smith is down at one of the saloons," replied Walt.

"Want I should go fetch him?" asked Ezra.

"I'd consider it a favor," replied Walt. "While you do that, I'll put our friend behind bars if I can find the cell door keys."

As Ezra hurried back up the street toward the saloons, Walt took Wells by an arm, guided him up onto the board-walk, and pushed the door open. The room was pitch black, so Walt struck a match. He guided Wells further into the room and lit a lantern swinging from the ceiling.

Seeing the ring of keys on the marshal's desk, he took those and pushed Wells through a door in the rear to the cells. Seeing Wells inside a cell, he swung the door closed and locked it. Wells sank to a bunk, glared at Walt a final time, then stretched out and lay down.

Moments later, Ezra returned with Richard Courtney.

"I asked for the marshal, not the banker," Walt said.

"We have a slight problem," Courtney replied. "A couple of W–in–a–B men came busting in here earlier. They told Marshal Smith what happened at the ranch. The marshal turned in his badge and left town with them hardly an hour ago. I've been looking around for someone to take his place, but I haven't hit on anyone yet. How about you, Walt?"

"Not me," Walt replied firmly. "I got tired of wearing a badge a long time ago. I'm not about to pin one on again."

"Just until we can find someone else?" Courtney asked, almost pleading.

"Well . . ."

"Good!" the banker said. Reaching into a desk drawer, he pulled out a marshal's badge. "Consider yourself sworn, and pin that on."

Reluctantly, Walt pinned the badge on.

"Have you got a place to sleep, Ezra?" Walt asked the cook.

"Don't worry about me," Ezra replied. "I'll find a place."

"There's an extra cell with a bunk back there," Walt told him. "You're welcome to use that."

"Why, thank you, Marshal," Ezra said and laughed. "Won't be the first time I slept in a jail."

"I'll be at the hotel if anything comes up," Walt said and left the office with Courtney on his heels.

"There's something else I need to tell you," the banker said when they were outside.

Walt, not liking the tone of Courtney's voice, pulled up short. "What?" he asked.

"The Reverend Pickering saw your young friend Tony on the street earlier today. He had Marshal Smith help him pick the boy up from the hotel. They took the boy to the orphanage. Said you hadn't the authority to keep Tony anyway. The way Tony was fighting, I expect they had to lock him up to keep him."

"Why those . . . !"

"What're you gonna do?" Courtney asked, a little alarmed at Walt's angry reaction.

"I'm marching up to that orphanage and getting Tony," Walt said.

"I know a way that would give you some leverage," Courtney said. "I hold a mortgage on the buildings up there, and the reverend is behind several months on his payments. That mortgage authorizes me to sell the buildings if the reverend gets behind in his payments. Why don't you buy the orphanage building?"

"How much?" asked Walt.

"If I have to foreclose, I could let the place go for a thousand dollars" replied Courtney.

"When can I take possession?" asked Walt.

"Come along with me," replied Courtney and chuckled. "I can sign those papers over to you at once. I'd like to see the reverend's face when he finds out you're the new owner of the orphanage. He's dealt with kids so long he's probably forgotten what it's like to come up against grownups."

"His way of dealing with kids is to beat and starve them," Walt said. "Tony told me all about conditions there. That's why he ran away every chance he got."

"I've heard rumors to that effect myself," the banker replied.

Walt decided he ought to tell Misty where he was going before he left town, so he headed for the hotel.

There was no reply when he knocked on Misty's hotel room door. He waited a moment and knocked again. Suddenly, the door was flung open, and Walt was staring into the muzzle of the Smith and Wesson .38 he'd bought her.

"Oh, I'm sorry!" Misty said and lowered the gun. "I thought you might be the marshal and that preacher coming back."

"I heard about what happened," Walt said.

"I did every thing I could to stop them."

"I don't doubt it, but I'll have Tony back one way or another today. I'm leaving for the orphanage now."

"Then I'll come with you!"

"Be best if you stayed here," Walt replied. "I don't know what will happen when I confront Pickering." Misty reluctantly agreed.

Stopping by the bank, Walt picked up the papers which showed he was the legal owner of Happy Land Orphanage.

"Mind if I ride along with you?" asked Courtney. "I want to see the reverend's face when he sees that paper."

"I think everything will go easier if I'm alone," replied Walt, "but thanks for the offer."

Chapter Twenty-four

Ace Hawley knew that as long as either Evan Wells or Misty lived, he would never gain control of the W–in–a–B. The time to strike, he thought to himself, was while Evan Wells was in jail. Still, he hesitated to do anything while Walt Davis was around. Then, to his surprise, he saw Davis leave the hotel and climb aboard his gelding. Turning the big horse into the street, Davis touched his knees to the horse's sides and sent him in an unhurried gallop along Main Street and out of town. Hawley's satisfaction knew no bounds.

"The time has come," he muttered.

First, he'd take care of Wells, then he'd see to the girl. Swinging aboard his mount, a sleek black gelding, he sent the animal into the alley and pulled up at the rear of the hotel. A small porch extended from the hotel doorway, and he wrapped the black's rein around the porch railing.

Hawley had a youngster waiting to whom he'd paid a dollar to deliver a note to Misty. Emerging once again on Main Street, he signaled to the boy and watched him enter the hotel. Hawley could hardly hold himself to a stroll as he headed for the jail. As though he had business there, he walked boldly into the office and found it empty, as he'd known he would. Drawing his six-gun, he passed through the office to the cells.

"About time you came for me!" Wells said, rising from the bunk and crossing to the cell door.

Wells' voice disturbed Ezra Dudley, who slept in the next cell. Wondering who Wells was talking to, Ezra lifted his head for a look.

"I ain't come for you, old man," Hawley said. "I come to kill you."

"To kill me?" exclaimed Wells. "Why, Ace? Didn't I always pay you good money?"

"I'll tell you why!" Hawley replied angrily. "You let me do all the killing, and you reaped all the gravy! Everybody thinks you're a big shot, but you wouldn't have been nothing if not for me!"

"I'll give you half of everything I've got, Ace! Just don't kill me!"

"You'd pay me a measly hundred dollars a month for the rest of my life!" Hawley yelled, taking aim at Wells.

"Even if you kill me, you won't get the ranch," Wells said. "My niece, Misty, is my next of kin. Everything will go to her."

"I got plans for Miss Prissy too," Hawley said. "I'll be picking her up after I leave here."

"You leave Misty alone!" Ezra Dudley yelled before he realized he had spoken.

Hawley was surprised by the yell. Turning, he recognized Dudley. "You're always getting in my way, old man," he said. Turning the gun on Dudley, he squeezed off a shot. The bullet creased Ezra's head and knocked him from the bunk. Hawley sent his second shot into Evan Wells' chest. Certain the shots would bring men running,

Hawley moved swiftly to the back door. Once outside, he raced along the back alley toward the back of the hotel.

Misty heard a timid tap on her door. Reaching for the pistol and, holding it behind her, she opened the door. She felt a little silly when she saw who was there.

"Are you Miss Wells?" asked a boy.

"Yes."

"I was told to give you this," the boy said. He gave Misty the note and hurried back downstairs.

Misty unfolded the note.

Misty,
Meet me at the rear of the hotel. I have news of Tony.
Walt.

Misty, worried about Tony and feeling guilty that she was responsible for letting Pickering take him, didn't stop to wonder why Walt hadn't come upstairs to see her. Grabbing a jacket, she hurried downstairs to the lobby and along the hallway to the back door. As she stepped outside, Ace Hawley grabbed her and clamped a hand over her mouth.

"You give me any trouble, I'll snap your neck," he whispered in her ear.

Unable to speak, Misty shook her head in agreement. Then she surprised Hawley with a sudden push and sent him sprawling.

Hawley muttered a curse. Reaching out, he caught Misty by her leg, bringing her down on top of him. He had already wasted too much time, he thought to himself and, giving Misty a swift cuff to her jaw, felt her go limp. Throwing her over his shoulder, he ran for the tethered black. He lifted Misty up before the saddle and, holding her in place, climbed aboard behind her, resting her head on his shoulder. Then he rode quietly along the alley. When he was free of the buildings, he touched spurs to the black and headed in the direction of the W–in–a–B, feeling as though he already had control of the ranch.

The Happy Land Orphanage occupied what had once been the Blackwell place, and some folks still called it that. Jay Blackwell, who had outlived all of his heirs, had left the large home to the town in his will to be used as they saw fit. The town fathers had promptly turned the property over to Reverend Pickering to be used as a badly needed orphanage.

An early cold front had already touched the range, and a continuing hot sun had turned the range a bleak brown. As Walt rode west toward the orphanage, he had a view of snowcapped mountains. The foothills closer in seemed to dance beyond curtains of hot air. The view reminded Walt of his stay in the mountains, and he found himself longing to return to the solitude he had enjoyed there.

The orphanage sat on a slight hill, and winds from the mountains whipped up small clouds of dust in the grass-less yard as Walt rode up. A couple of small boys in tat-tered overalls came from the barn and, bracing them-selves against the wind, walked to the house and entered. Apparently, they had seen the approaching rider and reported him, for the Reverend Pickering suddenly appeared on the front porch.

"Want to step down?" he invited as Walt pulled Cougar up before a hitch pole.

"Don't mind if I do," Walt replied, swinging down. Wrapping Cougar's rein about the pole, he climbed the steps to the porch. "I've come for my boy," he said as he faced the reverend.

"Which boy might that be?" asked Pickering.

"Tony Haskell. I believe you and the marshal took him by force from Miss Wells."

The reverend bristled. "You must be Walt Davis!"

"I am."

"You have no legal right to keep the boy!" he exclaimed. "He's a ward of the Happy Land Orphanage. Now, if you wish to apply for adoption, and you meet the requirements, something might be done."

"How long would such a thing take?"

"About six months, usually."

"Take a look at this," Walt said, extending the papers Courtney had given him.

As Pickering read, his face paled. "What's the meaning of this?" he demanded. "Richard Courtney wouldn't have sold the place out from under me!"

"I'm afraid he did, reverend. Now, produce the boy or get out."

"I won't!"

"Then I'll throw you off my property for trespassing. I'll also bring charges against you for abusing these children."

All the fight left Pickering, and his face turned gray as he sank into a chair. "If you let me stay, I'll never lay a hand on a child again!" he pleaded.

Despite his contempt for the cowering figure, and his anger at the man for his mistreatment of Tony, Walt couldn't help feeling a touch of pity for a man who seemed to be aging before his eyes. "Get up and take me to Tony!"

Trembling with fear, Pickering rose and led the way into the house. The front room was a large affair with several stuffed sofas filling up most of the space. All seemed to be leaking their innards. An assortment of children occupied the sofas and floor. They wore mostly rags and looked hungry and much too thin and lean, reminding Walt of the children in *Oliver Twist*. The children turned listless eyes on Walt with little curiosity as to his presence.

"Where is Tony?"

"He's in the next room."

"Lead me to him!"

Totally compliant to Walt's will now, Pickering led the way past the children to a door. Pushing the door open, he stepped back to let Walt enter. The room was bare of furniture, and faded green wallpaper hung in tatters from the walls. Even though the weather outside was warm, the room felt chilled. Tony sat in a corner of the room, his hands and feet tied, his eyes blindfolded.

Crossing quickly to him, Watt snatched the blindfold from his eyes. Tony's first reaction was to try and bite Walt's hand. Then his eyes blazed with happiness.

"I knowed you'd come!" he said.

Walt took a Barlow knife from his pocket and sliced through the ropes that bound Tony. Lifting the boy to his chest, he held him close for a moment. Releasing him, he said, "Let's get out of here, buddy."

Walt and Tony left the room but stopped amid the children in the front room and stared at their pathetic conditions. Watt was filled with frustration that there was nothing else he could do at the moment but leave the reverend in charge.

"When I get back to town," Walt told Pickering, "I'll ask Mr. Courtney at the bank to form a committee which will serve as a board of directors for the orphanage. I'm sure there are plenty of people who'll volunteer. I'll request the board come calling tomorrow. When they get here, you'll be out on your ear if this place and all the children aren't spotless, and the children had better be wellfed.

"If the board decides to let you stay, I'll personally come calling and check on the children from time to time. If I find you ever mistreat a child again, I won't be responsible for what I do to you. Is that clear to you, sir?"

"Yes, sir, very clear, and I thank you for your kindness!"

"Come on Tony. Let's get out of here."

Chapter Twenty-five

"You reckon Pickering will keep his word?" Tony asked on the ride back to town.

"I'll see to it," Walt replied, "but I expect the board of directors will keep a close eye on the reverend when they get a look at those children."

"I'm glad," Tony said. "Might not be such a bad place then."

"Are you saying you'd like to stay there?"

"Not on your life," Tony said and gave Walt a tight squeeze about his waist.

Happy to be reunited, Walt and Tony continued their ride into town and pulled up before the marshal's office.

"I need to check on Ezra and Mr. Wells," Walt said. "Wait here for me."

"Sure," Tony replied. Swinging from the saddle and holding Cougar's rein, he sat on the edge of the boardwalk and watched the few people of Prentiss who had ventured out.

Entering the marshal's office, Walt remembered that Ezra had decided to get some sleep in the extra cell. He decided to wake him and entered the cell block. He saw

Wells' crumpled figure first. Then something like a mutter came from the other cell, and he saw Ezra, face and shirt front bloody, struggling to stand. Dashing into the cell, he helped the old cook to the bunk and stretched him out.

"What happened here, Ezra?" he asked.

"Hawley!" Ezra whispered. "Ace Hawley! He shot me and then Wells. I guess his aim wasn't too good on me. The bullet just hit me in the head and knocked me cold."

"Why would he shoot Wells?" Walt asked, using his bandana to wipe Ezra's head clear of blood in order to see how serious the wound was. "I figured they were partners."

"Hawley wants the W-in-a-Box." Ezra said. "I heard him say as much."

"But the ranch will go to Misty," Walt said, "now that her uncle is dead . . . unless he left it to someone else."

"That's just it," Ezra exclaimed. "I heard Hawley say that when he left here, he'd be going for Misty. How is she? You make sure Hawley don't harm her!"

"I left her at the hotel," Walt said. The thought that Hawley might harm Misty struck fear in Walt's heart. "I'll send Tony to get Dr. Downs for you," he said to Ezra and then rushed from the cell, through the office, and outside. "Ezra's been hurt! Get Dr. Downs!" he said to Tony as he grabbed Cougar's reins and swung into the saddle.

"Where are you going?" Tony shouted, but Walt was pushing Cougar hard down the street and didn't hear him.

Pulling up before the hotel, Walt sprang from the saddle and rushed inside. "Have you seen Miss Wells?" he asked Sam Mitchell, the clerk.

"As a matter of fact, I have," replied Mitchell. "A boy came with a note for her. I sent him upstairs, and a few minutes later Miss Wells came down. She seemed in something of a hurry and went out the back way. Why? Is something wrong?"

Ignoring Mitchell's question, Walt raced along the hallway. Somehow Hawley had tricked her with the note into meeting him out back. Pushing the door open, he looked both ways along the alley and saw nothing. Then he noticed the scuff marks in the ground. He followed them to a spot where a horse had been tethered. From there, the horse's tracks headed west along the alley. The depth of the prints suggested the horse was carrying double.

Hawley's got her! The thought of what a man like Hawley might do to Misty left Walt reeling. He knew then that somehow over the past weeks the blond-haired, brown–eyed Misty Wells had come to mean the world to him. He loved her as he'd never loved a woman before. Turning, he ran back inside, stopping before the clerk's desk.

"Will you do me a favor?" he asked Mitchell, pausing a moment.

"Ask it."

"Do you know my boy, Tony?"

"Tony Haskell? The boy who was with Miss Wells?"

"Yes."

"Sure, I know him."

"I sent him for Dr. Downs to treat a wounded man at the jail. Go to the jail and tell Tony he's to stay here at the hotel till I get back. Put him in Miss Wells' room, and tell him if he doesn't stay there, I'll tan his hide. Will you do that?"

"Sure, Marshal," replied Mitchell, having heard of Walt's temporary appointment.

Satisfied that Tony would be taken care of, Walt hurried from the hotel to the street. Grabbing Cougar's reins, he swung into the saddle and rode down the alley to the rear of the hotel and picked up the trail and followed it out of town, surprised to find them heading in the direction of the W–in–a–Box. *Why is Hawley taking her to the ranch?* he asked himself.

Then, abruptly, the trail turned west toward the moun-

tains. Had something spooked Hawley? Had he discovered he was being followed? That thought concerned
Walt, because if Hawley had seen him, he would think
nothing of lying in wait to ambush him. If Hawley managed to kill him, what would happen to Misty? He
couldn't stand to consider that prospect.

With the Rockies for a background and the foothills
closer in, the trail led into a land of bare ground, stunted
sage, greasewood and mesquite, and often through
strange eroded rock formations. Gradually, the mesquite
was reduced to mere bushes, interspersed with clumps of
creosote and other thorny brush. However hard and rough
the terrain, Walt realized he was still on W–in–a–Box land,
where Hawley, no doubt, had ridden across many times
and knew only too well.

Suddenly, the tracks disappeared, and Walt noted the
stretch of rock-like clay ahead. Swinging down, he covered the hardpan on foot, leading Cougar, but as far as he
could see, nothing, not even an animal, had passed over
the ground recently. Ace Hawley's trail had disappeared
as completely as a whisper in a wind.

Walt took the only course open to him. He rode in ever
widening circles looking for tracks, growing more frustrated by the minute at the thought of what Misty might be suf-
fering. Then, a half mile from where he had lost the trail,
he picked up the tracks again. Breathing a sigh of relief and
hoping he wouldn't be too late, he took up the trail.

Obviously, Hawley thought he had shaken any pursuit,
for he now made no effort to hide his trail. Still, Walt was
at a disadvantage; he had no idea now how far ahead
Hawley was. He knew a little about judging the age of
tracks, but on a hard surface, the job was doubly difficult.

Crossing a patch of sand, he pulled Cougar up and
swung down. The age of tracks in sand, he recalled, was
easier to judge. Little or no sand would have dribbled

from the track's rim if the sand was damp and the tracks fresh. As tracks aged and dried out, more and more sand dribbled in. Walt was heartened when he saw the sides of the tracks were still intact. Hawley couldn't be more than thirty minutes ahead, maybe less.

The trail through the sand showed him something else as well. Hawley's horse was tiring. Before each print the animal had left a slight dragging sign, a sure indication that the horse was about played out. Hawley would have to stop and rest soon or he'd be walking.

The sun, hot and fiery, reached midway across the sky, turning even the thin Colorado air muggy. The smell of resin off a nearby hot cedar was strong. A small herd of antelope bounded away, white rumps flashing. A crow flew past overhead and bounced with each flap of his wings. Walt forced himself to concentrate on the tracks, afraid he might get distracted by his surroundings and lose the trail.

Ace Hawley, aware he was being followed, turned the black into the draw and rode toward a log cabin set among a small grove of trees. Pulling up before the cabin, he slid from the saddle and helped Misty down.

Misty's feet had hardly touched the ground when she began to fight, raking her fingernails across Hawley's face, leaving scratches severe enough to cleave the skin. Hawley cursed angrily and slapped her hard to the side of her head, knocking her unconscious again.

"That'll teach you to fight me!" he muttered and, grabbing a rope from the black's saddle, wrapped it around Misty, binding her feet tightly together and her arms at her side. He then used the ends of the rope to tie her upright to a small sapling growing next to the door. "A bit of cheese to bait the trap," he said and smiled his satisfaction. Then he led the black out among the oaks and tied him off to a low hanging limb. Taking his rifle from its scabbard, he settled down to wait, knowing the wait wouldn't be long.

Walt followed the trail to the mouth of the draw and, seeing the cabin beneath the trees, pulled up. He had the distinct feeling someone was watching him. He had neither seen nor heard anything, but he knew they were there. He had worn a badge long enough to know never to discount his intuition. Hunches, as they were often called, had saved the life of many a man, his included.

Then he saw the body tied to the sapling before the cabin. The blond hair falling from the bowed head could belong to no one but Misty. Throwing caution aside, he kneed Cougar, sending him in an urgent gallop toward the cabin. He was almost there when the first shot rang out from among the trees, and the thought flashed through his mind that he had foolishly ridden into the ambush he'd feared all along. Ace Hawley had set him up.

Cougar stumbled and went down, throwing Walt from the saddle. Landing on his back, Walt was breathless for a moment. He wanted to move, but knew if he made the slightest motion, he'd be a dead man. He forced himself to remain stock-still and, barely closing his eyes, managed to slip a furtive hand down to his holster and find it empty.

He heard the sound of feet approaching, and the click of a hammer being cocked. Then the gun appeared a foot or so above his head, followed by Hawley's face. "If you didn't break your neck, you're dead meat now, sucker," Hawley muttered, and Walt saw his finger tighten on the trigger.

He sprang into action. His first move was to knock the gun aside, surprising Hawley. The gun exploded, and the bullet slammed into the dirt where Walt's head had been. Grabbing for Hawley's legs, Walt managed to throw him aside before he could get off another shot and, scrambling to his feet, kicked the gun, knocking it from Hawley's hand. Hawley was on his feet by then, and the two circled each other warily.

Hawley's eyes had a savage, deadly look that Walt somehow found familiar. Then he remembered the mountain lion he'd faced back in the canyon. Hawley's eyes were black, the lion's yellow, but the message was the same. They were the eyes of a killer, an animal who had killed before, liked it, and wanted the thrill of killing again.

Hawley made the first move. Yelling curses, he charged, head first, knocked Walt backward, and landed on top of him, his hands searching for Walt's throat. Walt, slightly dazed from the head butt, fought desperately to throw Hawley aside. Then the gunman's long fingers closed around Walt's neck. Walt's hands found Hawley's wrist and he tried to break the hold. Failing, he slipped his hands up to Hawley's fingers and tried to pull them free. That effort was unsuccessful as well.

By then, the pain in his chest had begun to build, and he struggled again to break Hawley's hold, and again failed. Now the pain was like a dagger in his lungs, and he knew it would only be seconds until he blacked out. Where the idea came from, he would never know, but suddenly he lifted his legs high and wrapped them about Hawley's neck. With his remaining strength, he squeezed his knees into the gunman's neck, brought his legs down, taking Hawley, now gasping for breath himself, to his back, and holding him there, while the air rushing into his own lungs felt like liquid fire. Hawley made a mighty heave and freed himself. They came up simultaneously, both men sucking in oxygen.

Walt didn't wait for Hawley to make the first move this time. Stepping in, he sent a jab to the gunman's face.

Hawley threw his head back to dodge the jab, and Walt followed with a right to the gunman's belly. Hawley, hurt, still managed to counter with a blow to the side of Walt's head that made him see double for a moment.

Before he could recover, Hawley closed in and tried a thrust with his knee to Walt's groin that barely missed. He followed that with a head butt to Walt's chin that produced exploding lights before Walt's eyes. Shaking off the pain again, and before Hawley could step back, Walt landed a right to Hawley's face and felt the crunch of a broken nose.

Hawley gave a grunt of pain, fell backward, and made an effort to crawl away. Walt, almost spent, might have let him go, but saw he was headed for the gun Walt had earlier kicked from his hand. Calling upon some final inner strength, Walt pushed himself up and made a leap for Hawley's back, landing on him just as Hawley grabbed the gun, lifted it, and struggled to squeeze the trigger. The gun exploded before Walt's eyes, blinding him. The blast, like a crack of thunder inside his ears, left him deaf as well.

Several moments passed before a glow replaced the murky shade before Walt's eyes and light broke through. With ears still ringing, Walt pushed himself up. Ace Hawley lay beneath him, his shirt front wet with blood, a look of surprised agony frozen on the dead mask of his face.

Remembering Misty, Walt staggered to her and, managing to get the Barlow from his pocket, opened it, and cut her free, catching her to keep her from falling. Something, maybe the gentleness of Walt's arms, caused Misty's eyes to flutter open, and she looked up into his face.

"I knew you'd come," she managed.

"And I'll never go away again," Walt whispered, "if you'll let me stay."

Slowly her arms went about his neck. "Let's see how you kiss," she said, her voice stronger now.

Walt lowered his lips to hers in a long, gentle kiss, hoping the message in his heart came through. He broke the kiss and gazed into a pair of shining brown eyes. "Well?" he asked.

"You can stay if you do that again."

He did.